PAUL JOHN RADLEY

My Blue-Checker Corker and Me

TICKNOR & FIELDS · NEW YORK

1986

Copyright © 1982 by Paul John Radley
All rights reserved. No part of this work may be reproduced or transmitted in any form or by any means, electronic or mechanical, including photocopying and recording, or by any information storage or retrieval system, except as may be expressly permitted by the 1976 Copyright Act or in writing from the publisher. Requests for permission should be addressed in writing to Ticknor & Fields, 52 Vanderbilt Avenue, New York, New York 10017.

First American edition, 1986

Library of Congress Cataloging-in-Publication Data

Radley, Paul, 1962–
My blue-checker corker and me.
1. Pigeons—Fictions. I. Title.
PR9619.3.R22M9 1986   823   86-5778
ISBN 0-89919-432-X
ISBN 0-89919-472-9 (pbk.)

Printed in the United States of America

V 10 9 8 7 6 5 4 3 2 1

MY BLUE-CHECKER CORKER
AND ME

ALSO BY
PAUL JOHN RADLEY

Jack Rivers and Me

For
BOBBIE RADLEY

who grew up in Australia in the thirties in the world of the "Hollywood Saturday Matinee," who married a GI, Kenny Betts, during World War II and went to the United States with him, where she spent the rest of her life raising five daughters and working for RCA Victor in Findlay, Ohio. She never lost her belief in her dream of the American Dream.

"Our ideas and our instincts work upon our memory of these people who have lived before us, and so they take some clarity of outline. It's not to our credit to think we begin today, and it's not to our glory to think we end today. All through time we keep coming into the shore like waves. You stick to your blood, son; there's a certain fierceness in blood that can bind you with the long community of life."

Stark Young, *So Red the Rose*

It isn't easy to resurrect a place that exists farther away than dreams: only memories can afford the frail embellishments. This is the excuse I offer for the melded topographic lies and surrendering anachronisms.

This book could not have been written without the support of my mother, Janice, who loved five kids through the insanity of childhood to the unquiet peace of their safer, somewhat selves . . .

without the encouragement of Niels Stevens, who has motivated young Australians to mold imagination for the pleasure of others . . .

without the baton of Beatrice Davis, who deals in truth . . .

nor without the guidance of Canada Jack, a perennial old bastard, who told me so much about the enduring pigeons my great-grandfather, Big Dar, flew throughout his resolute life that I feel I have lived before in a dulcet, richer but poorer world . . . and I regret that I haven't.

MY BLUE-CHECKER CORKER
AND ME

Visa

BETWEEN THE WINDSHORN Booradeela Range and the low-flung foothills of Mount Kaiser there is a mild sweep of earth. These roving Terribana Hills roll eastward and down from the Dividing Range towards the South Pacific to the mothering waters of a lake and their gullies cross the valley with limping streams that spill into Dooragul Creek which drains into this same pleasant Lake MacDonald.

About thirty crow miles from the beetling, fluted forehead of the mountain is the ocean entrance to the lake at Boolawoy Beach; almost midway between lies the lowest spot in the valley, a mud flat called Tuggeroo Wash where the Dooragul wades into MacDonald.

And there you have it in the palm of your mind . . . Lillipilli Valley, New South Wales, Australia. Up from Down Under all over. A small mellow world; and the people born here imagined this *was* the world.

It was a peaceful life, and the natives and other creatures living there existed in a semi-belligerent contentment.

"You mean . . ."

I mean belt up and listen.

Maybe this place is still to be found in another place,

tucked away in a tideless summer where leaves never fall and memories and emotions are as fluid as time, where men and women never aspire to any heaven beyond their hearts.

"God willin' an' if the fuckin' creek don't rise!"

Take this signal morning, some numbered year when Korea was still in the news and World War II was distilled news. One token town, Boomeroo, is yawning beneath a sky of September hue. The moon is ghosting in the wan sunlight as though caught in the jealous vise of night. The young sun is already promising a world of warmth without end. A breeze is interpreting some soul symphony in the schoolground wattles. The willows wading down the storm-water channel are taking communion, still strung with rosaries of weeping dew.

There is no other gossip on the air. Call it the correcting moment: a town is a clock and winding helps.

Why not grasp this unpolluted moment out of time? Any captured fraction of it has the quality of infinity, so grab it now: you might have all the immunity of eternity in your soul but your spendable years are short.

"Oh well, I guess we live and learn by rumbum rules."

"Miss Cruikshank always said when you learnt something you lost something else."

Actions still mean more than prayers here, but any calamity will find them muttering fervently for help: Oh God, don't hate me for what I've done wrong . . . love me for what I'm tryin' to do right!

1

THIS IS the encompassing world of Richard Montgomery Howard, a twelve-year-old schoolboy now reading aloud at the breakfast table before whipping off to a wild day at the Boomeroo Public School: "This wide brown land is an island-continent of asphalt arteries and half-mapped membranes; a lonely big body between wide seas and beneath far stars."

"Sounds like a pommy book," his hovering Grandad said, rattling a huge English china breakfast cup.

"Sounds like Big Fat Nellie swimmin' in the creek on a hot night," Monte said. "Wish we had ashfelt in the school playground, but."

"Asphalt," Grandad said. "I thought Miss Cruikshank had you out of the habit of ending your sentences with 'but.' "

"Like you just did?" Monte said.

"Smartarse," his grandfather said.

Mount Kaiser is a geographical tyrant and shadows the district with jagged peaks recalling the force of massive dawn eruptions. Time has never succeeded in softening the barren rockface rising from scrubless shoulders where not even wallabies retreat.

Snarling south, the Booradeela Range looks like a challenge from the lower flexure of the valley, but from the keen floating eye of a hawk it seems cast off from the other ranges where it allows Oxford Pass to fossick through to the west — and pigeons to home from the northwest.

The Terribana Hills crouch beneath Ol' Man Kaiser and cover their pale green crotches with patches of interlocking lantana whose tiny multicolored flowers confetti the summer. These hills spread a pretense of grass where no more than three or four inches of despairing soil hide their gravel guts. On drier slopes weeds give way to rashes of tick-ridden tea-tree scrub.

"They may not be the softest hills in the world," the teacher, Mark Griffith, said returning from a Japanese prisoner-of-war camp, "but they sure's hell satisfy the lump in your throat."

" 'Ey, just listen to this, Grandad," Monte said. " 'Australians are harsh, rooted characters' . . . I thought 'rooted' was a dirty word."

"Not when it means like roots of a tree."

". . . 'with evasive hearts but ten . . . tenable minds.' Crickey!"

"People don't see other people in a mirror, Boy," Grandad said.

"Granfarver Jones hates Pommies," the boy said. "Says they sent us here bloody convicts."

"Our ancestors *were* convicts," the old man said, blotting out the "bloody" with his eyes. "Just remember your Dad died fighting for the British as well as us."

"I gotta go," Monte said with a scrap of voice, his heart too suddenly filled with the poetry of Dad, William Richard Howard, sometimes remembered as Boy Howard because he, too, had been a swimming champion like Boy

Charlton . . . only sorta not as famous. Often recalled as Bill, but mostly called Chid by oldtimers because as a nipper he ran around naked when Chidley was still well remembered.

"Chidley? Grandad?"

"He was a health fanatic. Went round in a tunic. Talked freely about sex. Was ahead of his time."

Monte hesitated in the back doorway as the old fellow began to clear the dishes from the morning newspaper which they always used as a breakfast cloth. "By the by, Grandad, what does 'tenable' mean?"

The old man smiled, illuminating the love teaming them. "Thought you'd get round to that. Well . . . I read about a castle once that held out in a long siege. It was hard to conquer and was called 'tenable.' "

The kid hoisted his bag. "Oh!" He soccered with an old pot near the door. "You think I maybe have a sort of tenable mind?"

"Ya bloody hard to beat in an argument if that's what you're getting at," Grandad said over his shoulder. "Now get off to school before you're later than you already are."

Monte went off with a host of childhood expressions exercising his eyes: the product of a country town that sat shabbily in the throat of the valley, throttled between a cement works and a coalmine, glorified only by retreating shreds of nature and guarded joyously by the assailants of the bar in the local pubs.

"It's nice, ain't it, livin' here among all ya friends?"

"Why, you grub, you could count your friends on a fish's fingers."

"Bullshit. I got friends. Lots of 'em. Right here in fuckin' Boomeroo. More friends than you could whack your dick at."

"Anyone says they got more friends than enemies is kiddin' 'emselves . . . even in Boomeroo."

These drinkers believed relentlessly in their local holy

and in the Boomeroo Bulls who sang, when they were on the piss after a Rugby Union game, about this bloody beautiful town:

> "*Boomerooooh . . . Boomerooooh . . .*
> *On the bloody beautiful bloody*
> *banks of beautiful bloody . . .*
> *Dooragul-bloody-Creek.*"

Win or lose the Union players sing into the drunken hours of Saturday night for as long as they can support one another in evading the clutch of wives and shift of sheilas in the ladies' lounge.

"In some pubs in Sydney they let women drink in the bar now."

"Shit, who cares? Who wants to live anywhere 'cept in Boomeroo."

"That's probably what the coalmine cocker-roaches say."

"It's cockroach, you prick-wit, not cocker-roach!"

"If I wanta say cocker-fuckin'-roach I'll say fuckin' cocker-roach."

Of course, Dooragul Creek isn't really so bloody beautiful.

"Maybe not, but the lake sure is."

This is very true. Lake MacDonald is honestly fucking beautiful, although it's more lagoon than lake.

A broad shimmer of caught water which the Pacific Ocean refreshes each year after winter storms have washed away the umbilical beach strand at Boolawoy, this lake is a haven for fish and men. The spring tides doctor the ravished sand until, come surprising summer, the surf is up again.

It is shaped by fingers and thumbs of land and played upon by green ripples except where a rough heel of blue water washes west along the south shore. This is Wessouthern Bay, and in the grip of a bedouin wind it will protest for the whole imprisoned lagoon.

Tuggeroo fishermen who rent their smacks to Sunday sightseers heading for the bay have a taut warning: "Careful ya don't catch yer balls in a squall."

Last bell has gone and the schoolkids have armied indoors. A North-West Express has furrowed its rowdy way through the valley, stopping impatiently at Boomeroo to let off steam and pick up the shadows of travellers, and refill its water tank.

"Th' expresses won't be stopping here much longer. Diesels will soon be hauling all the fast trains."

" 'Ow would you know? All you got is a diesel dong an' you don't even work on the rotten railway."

"Somebody *works* on the railway?"

Most of the shops will soon be opening but the butcher has been trading for hours because he was up at 4 A.M. *to* go to the Winchester Abattoirs.

"Like to get there early an' get the best cuts for me customers, Mrs. Allsop." His eyes were usually so shining sharp he could have carved with them.

"I'd rather have a good cut off the price, Mr. Sprinks!"

The exultant cage-wheel at the pithead across the creek is hesitant, and on the hilly perimeter of the town the cement works are temporarily basking: it's smoko.

The post-breakfast back-fence chatter is over and housewives are inside swimming through cereal dishes, porridge plates, toast platters, eggcups, teacups and saucers.

"Don't stand on ceremony at breakfast, Beulah; don't give'm saucers . . . or you might find out by dinner time they're goin'ta want the carpet their mothers rolled out for 'em."

The little people in the Infants School have not yet begun to chant their invincible version of "Lavender's Blue, Dilly Dilly."

"Who's this Dilly Dilly the little drongos sing about? Some Abo?"

Soon some peerless boy will hoof it down a back street with a matchboxful of slim black bushflies — to dip in ink and drop on a girl's neat page — and attack his teacher with grim lies rather than with an honest excuse or a note for being late. The Catholic schoolchildren will erupt audaciously from the placidity of Mass. An abrasive motorist will drive upon the Co-op Store in a fanfare of gears and brakes.

"To get something on appro, I bet."

The postman will abruptly start punishing his whistle.

"Blowin' that thing like it's Judgment Day . . . he'll end up bustin' his poofa valve!"

Mrs. Allsop, a wound-up woman of this and many other years, her hennaed hair a geodesic masterpiece of bobby pins, will rule her way along Main Road like Britannia in Dublin. She's on her way to scandal command at the butcher's . . .

"The ceiling fan keeps the flies away and the sawdust is easy on the feet, Maisie, if you want to stand around and kill time."

. . . to murder reputations, refute opinions, bestow household hints and pare skeleton secrets at random and never rued.

"I told you, Val, to wear your cardigan inside out at home. Keeps it clean on the right side in case you have to dash out in a hurry."

Mrs. Allsop knows more about nothing than Plato and less about everything than Mrs. Malaprop. "Listen *hear* . . ."

And that's exactly how she means it.

". . . Gloria: I can tell by the way these young tabbies fiddle with their engagement rings if they're getting it or not. The way they fondle it gives them away. Thinkin' about sex all the time, it seems."

"And some of them gettin' it all the time, too, nowadays. Ain't the young ones lucky?"

Even smoko at the cement works, as resilient as it is, can't be stretched for ever.

"That's what you think, mate."

A happy young shiftworker will rev his new motorbike with loving energy. Not far away his aching, forsaken girlfriend will play the wireless louder to let him know how little she cares about his mechanical mistress.

And if heaven doesn't fall Granfarver Jones will rouse himself from the rocking chair and announce to all and sundry in his disjointed household, "I'm goin' down the back yard for me mornin' poop."

Near by, as he rambles to the distant dilapidated lavatory, old Granny Green's ageless white cockatoo will screech at her, "Time-to-shit-time-to-shit!"

"You dumb cockie. The world ain't comin' to an end just because that old fool's goin' to the dunny."

Grandfather Singleton — Monte's Grandad — will take his pipe down to the pigeon ducket and scoot all Monte's birds up for their morning training fly. He'll watch them skim the ceiling of Boomeroo like a charm of cherubim, recalling his own flying days, remembering certain birds that helped make him a widely known fancier and valley authority on racing pigeons. In about forty minutes he'll beckon them home with his familiar whistle and they'll respond immediately, like well-loved children who know that no harm can possibly come to them in this their own timeless world.

"Time isn't a plague feeding on those predestined to fill its appetite, children," the Public School Headmistress said to Sixth Class at the beginning of their last primary year. "It's a gorgeous vehicle that will take you as far as you decently want to go."

"Miss Cruikshank? 'Predestined'?"

"Elizabeth Griffith, explain the word 'predestined' to Kenneth Leslie."

"Yes, Miss Cruikshank."

Five minutes later Elizabeth was still embroiled in a gory history of Marie Antoinette. Saving the French Queen from a fate worse than the guillotine and little kinder than death, the teacher intervened saying, "I only wanted the pith of it, Elizabeth."

" 'Pith,' Miss Cruikshank?"

"Pith-off," Duck Allsop whispered and raised a few giggles from close-by kids who had heard that yarn.

"Francis Drake Allsop!" the Headmistress said. She also knew how to hurt. Pronouncing her words solemnly, she told Duck, "Tonight you will write out one hundred times: 'Pith means gist.' "

Brave immemorial woman, Kate Cruikshank. It is indecent to remember how little she received in those days for the imagination she gave to teaching, the glory she brought to learning, and the patience she offered to classes of over forty pupils. Her species is extinct: she is gone not just for now but for the rest of man's belonging. A beautiful, ugly old dinosaur of a woman with a brain like Galileo's, a heart not unlike Spinoza's and the unremitting courage of an Emily Pankhurst.

How could you ever forget the day she said, "Children, it's a sad fact, but you must learn to accept the life you have before you ask: 'Which way is the world?' "

Yet in all that lifetime only one person, a little girl called Callie Gordon, ever told her: "I love you, Miss Cruikshank."

2

RESTLESS, HEFTY GRAY clouds assembled over Boolawoy waiting for a creative elbow of wind from the ocean, their shapes charged with movement. It came from the north...

"That weather man on the wireless ain't often right but he's wrong again."

... and instead of brushing them up the Lillipilli in charcoal droves it spread them south toward the great gutter of the Hunter River Valley. Exposing their fat undersides, they shuffled after one another like airborne elephants. An immense free cloudy circus.

Arnie Holman swung on the schoolbell rope like a flying possum and a flood of kids were flushed from the school corridors. Duck Allsop wrenched tiny Arnie from his bell-swing. "Give it 'ere, ya drongo. I'll showya how to ring the stinkin' guts outa the bloody thing." Arnie didn't wait for the demonstration which undoubtedly would have ended in a larruping.

Amid the counterflow of escaped scholars Monte walked home with Jerry Kyle who lived in the brothel next door. His other mates had been kept in for farting aloud deliberately.

"Those clouds look like Hannibal crossing the Alps, Jerry."

Jerry nodded. The good thing about Kylie was he understood things with an instinct that mattered to you. Monte didn't care that people talked about Jerry's Mum the same way they ridiculed Big Fat Nellie. He was childishly, innately tolerant.

"If some people's tongues had hindsight they'd see a whole sight better," Grandad said.

Young Peterdan Kerr followed them across Scots Street and down Harrow. In front of Monte's place he asked if he could help feed the pigeons.

"You better go home today, Peterdan," Monte said. "I got some younguns I don't want disturbed yet." Monte was probably the only kid in town who didn't call him Li'l Peterdunny, which Gloamy Lightfoot had invented after he had learnt from the town Yank, Tony Delarue, that a prick was a peter.

"Know what the balls said to the judge?"

"What?"

"Why should we do the hangin' . . . it was Peter done the shootin'!"

Li'l Peterdunny's life had been difficult ever since. "Well, don't forget it's my turn to help polish the showroom," he muttered humbly.

"OK. See you Sunday morning," Monte said.

"Well . . . 'ooroo, you two."

"So long," Monte said.

"Ta-ta," Jerry said placatively, then added, "Now you go straight home, Li'l Peterdunny. Your Mum worries the way you wander."

Monte had a restricted gang: Terry Madison, Gloamy Lightfoot and Batter Rees, who helped him polish the linoleum floor of Mr. Canwell's car showroom every Sunday morning. Their differences complemented one another's without preventing them from sharing interests: the tough young awesome beauty of Terry; the gangling wariness of Batter; the frightening spontaneity of Gloamy. When it suited him, Monte could find himself in their combustion or lose himself in his own element.

Cleaning the large expanse of linoleum was worth five shillings...

"Sure beats hell outa Sunday School!"

... and Monte had begun the job when he was nine. He found it a lonely, aching experience.

"It's like polishing a bloody big paddock of lino, Grandad. If he didn't park all the cars outside on Sunday and I only had to polish around them it wouldn't be so bad."

"The Presbyterian church is just round the corner if you want to go back to Sunday School," Grandad said. "You just can't run the streets on Sunday."

"I know. Aw... guess I couldn't let Mr. Canwell down at this stage of me fame. Not now I got it all organized."

"Didn't think you could," Grandad said, winking one side of his mouth. "I hear you don't do too much work up there yourself any more."

On Sunday early in the piece, Jerry Kyle had gone along to help, and devised the skating gig. They tied the polishing rags to their feet and skated the shine on in record time, to the tune of the hymns being sung in the Presbyterian church.

Later Monte got Feet-Feet Anderson, who shared the front rooms of Vonnie Kyle's house with another whore, Angela Withers (the Ten-bob Angel), to sew polishing cloths to fit their feet like sloppy slipper-flippers. Everybody enjoyed the final hymn best because the Sunday School kids, earnest to be done with goodness for the week, rollicked through it and the skaters could really get stuck into their top finish.

This had become the most exclusive sport in Boomeroo

and Monte had an embarrassingly long waiting list of workers. Each Sunday at midday Mr. Canwell came by to run the cars back in and pay Monte. He was a good old man with a spare grin and a bear hug . . .

"But he ain't a poofter like Old Mr. Rowlandson."

"Old Rowlandson ain't really a poofter," Swiftie Madison once said with almost-feeling. "He's a two-way sucker! He sucks an' 'e gets sucked in."

. . . an additional joke and an extra sixpence for the odd boys helping out that day. Then they hot-footed it along to the paper shop and bought frozen oranges, rum-and-milk caramels and a couple of bottles of the new favorite drink, Coca-Cola, which even Mrs. Allsop had recently given her loud experienced blessing.

"It's the only decent thing the Yanks left here after the war, except their kids . . . but they ain't patented yet. Coke helps you belch, too, Muriel, if you've got wind."

"Too bad it don't do the same for a pain in the arse like Mum Allsop."

The gang would settle down on the concrete gutter-step in front of the paper shop and tell yarns—some clean, some shoofty. They'd also yak about cowboy pictures and compare the legends of Hollywood and the Wild West with their own colonial heroes. Time and place were immaterial to their roving imaginations. They had stream-of-consciousness instincts, and the past and present and future were bottled, ready to be poured quickly, decanted slowly, or rebottled. They might stack Ben Hall up against Jesse James; John Wayne versus Ned Kelly; Frank Gardiner meets Billy the Kid. The new rage from *Red River*, Montgomery Clift (alias Matthew Garth), runs into Jack Donahoe, the Wild Colonial Boy.

They had their idols and hates, but one man remained irrevocably alone: Ben Hall. Any kid who didn't understand that was an ill-educated drongo. It sometimes seemed that if God was as lucky as He was Almighty He too was in the same heaven as Ben Hall.

"Ben Hall . . . looked up to bah all," Tony Delarue once said in his deliberately worst, overhauled American accent. The marooned Yank who had married the local girl was usually hell-bent to be an Aussie but sometimes his natural gut-juices got the better of his tact.

"The Yanks don't understand, but! They even make heroes outa sheriffs."

"Didya hear the one Mr. Delarue tells about the hurricane and the coconut palm? 'Hang onto ya nuts . . . this is no ordinary blow job!' "

"I like the one about Pat and Mick when Mick's watch stopped. Well . . . Pat said he'd fix it an' takes the floggin' thing to pieces, an' finds a dead fly inside. 'Bejesus, Mick,' he says, 'no wonder the friggin' thing won't go . . . the bloody engine driver's dead.' "

"Duck tells a good yarn, don't 'e?"

"Specially the one about the drunk who goes into the pub and gets a beer. He drinks some then says to the barmaid, 'This is piss.' So he orders another one an' when she brings that back he sips it then pours it on the bar and says to her again, '*Piss!*' Then she gets the manager who comes over to the drunk and says, 'Piss off, mate!' The old drunk grins and says, 'That's great . . . *now* I'll have a beer.' "

The wake of laughter never betrayed a weak joke or how many times a particular story had been heard before. That would be as bad as skiting about how many clippings you had of Ben Hall, or how many times you'd seen *Red River*.

"What about the two little drongos goin' home from school and come across a dirty big dog turd. One of them picks it up and says, 'Looks like dog shit,' then hands it to the other. He smells it and says, 'Smells like dog shit,' and hands it back. Then that one squeezes it and says, 'Feels like dog shit,' and passes it back again. This time the second little drongo takes a bite and says, 'Tastes like dog shit.' Then the one who picked it up takes it again and says, 'Lucky we didn't walk in it.' "

This was mateship in the womb of boyhood: and the fierce birth of that monstrous fetus of terrible beauty — Australian chauvinism — would burst upon young men a few years later in a manhood abounding in beer. This bond took decades to fade and sometimes, between some men, it never died. No woman ever found an effective weapon against it.

"Mum! It don't matter if he's right or wrong. He's in trouble and he's me cobber!"

Marriage did not diminish it.

"Put anovver steak on, luv! Me mate Shagger's come for tea. He's 'ad a blue wiff his missus, an' he's gonna let 'er sweat it out for a few hours."

"They'll never make another cowboy picture like *Red River*."

"Or fix another fight as good as the one between John Wayne and Montgomery Clift. Was you called after him, Howdie?"

"No. After some British General. But I wrote to Montgomery Clift and he sent me a signed picture . . . the one where he's wearin' that beaut dirty suede jacket."

"I didn't like that sheila that tried to latch onto him, but. 'Matthew, Matthew!' " Swiftie Madison could mimic Joanne Dru with a professional unimportance.

"Heck, me either. I was glad when she copped that arrow in the tits."

Someone always said that. You could bet your storebought teeth on it. And if you didn't know about Walter Brennan and his store-bought teeth then you were due to end up in Purgatory with the Lone Ranger, Hopalong

Cassidy and all those smiling sing-along cowboys who never knew girls had twats.

It seemed unnecessary to amend the rites of youth.

"How you reckon Tom Dunstan would go against Thunderbolt?"

Someone always asked that and someone else always had a colt-quick reply. You could hitch your horse to it.

"I reckon Matthew Garth would give Johnnie Gilbert a run for his gun."

"Gilbert was a flash cove!"

"And shot his own uncle. Matthew Garth woulda let Tom Dunstan drill him insteada drawin' against him . . . that was gutsy . . ."

"An' only John Wayne could get away with pretendin' he was goin' to kill Monte Clift."

"Yeah!!"

Oh, what the hell? If you've never had Red-Riveritis there's no way of explaining the ins-and-outs of these crosswise conversations rewrapped a hundred times in the intensity of that innocence which precedes the intent of love.

"See you," Jerry said with a farewell tap on the shoulder as they walked down the common gravel driveway between their houses.

Monte half-saluted. As he bolted up the back steps he heard Mrs. Kyle's power of words.

"Dawdling home from school again, you lazy little who'aah! Jerry, you know I got jobs waiting for you after school."

He could feel sorry for Jerry, but in some genderless way he liked Vonnie Kyle. Her voice stirred responses in him. And she always smelt good, like new. Feet-Feet, who was a lot younger and friendlier, was sweaty and smelt old. The Ten-bob Angel wasn't very accessible at all.

Once Monte had seen Jerry's mother (in a rare mood)

cuddling him and had enjoyed imagining himself locked in those cool white mother arms. He burst in upon Grandad.

"Grandad, what's a who'aah?"

"A whore." Grandad was unflinching.

"Like in hoar frost?"

"No. Like in double-you-aitch-oh-are-eee! Whore. Woman who likes a lot of men and takes money for . . . the pleasure and relief she gives them."

"Like a slut and all the dogs mounting her."

"A bit," Grandad said in a quick-stitch tone indicating this conversation was about to be sewn up.

"But Jerry's a boy."

"Oh . . . well, Vonnie Kyle's like a lot of people when they want to hurt someone and say the first worst thing that comes to mind. It doesn't mean she don't love Jerry. Most likely means she hates herself. Now, you got any homework you can do tonight and not at the breakfast table in the morning?"

"Gee, Grandad, there's more to life than doin' everything licketty-split."

"Maybe, Boy, but if I don't watch you you're goin' to be putting off till tomorrow what you should've done yesterday."

At Allsop's, Duck was fixing a hinge to a loose paling on Alderton's fence so that he could let his dirty big black retriever into the neighbor's fowlhouse.

"And what did you learn at the Public School the nuns couldn't've taught you?"

Mr. Allsop wasn't an indulgent father but was so pleased to come home from work and find his son fixing the falling fence he spoke more pleasantly than he usually did.

"That Australians are a lot of rooted buggers, Dad," Duck said. "Oh . . . and that 'gith' means 'pissed.' I gotta write that out tonight!"

"'Gith' means 'pissed,' does it?" His Dad couldn't remember that one. "Bet the nuns never taught you anything dirty like that."

"No, but they used to whang the crap outa me," Duck said. "Old Cruikshank, she don't hit you with nothin' but words."

The next day Mrs. Allsop said to a cornered neighbor, "We might have to send our boy Duck back to the Catholic school, Marge. Kate Cruikshank's teaching him words only fit for the billiard room and the pub. By the way, did you know that 'gith' meant 'pissed'?"

Up and down and around the valley, the democracy of nature bends to and blends with this Saxon seed, blooming nowhere more noticeably than in Boomeroo. It's not that they really hate anybody: they simply like themselves more.

"Stiff-shit! I'm from Jindaboolawaringoondigi."

3

TUGGEROO IS THE weed-coated tongue of Dooragul Creek where the yearly swill from Boolawoy Beach ends up after the lake has sifted out the clean white sand from the winter outrage. Tuggeroo village is smelly, unpainted and blessedly unvarnished. Although it attracts arty-tarty tourists, it is real, not scenery, and the people who live there could be called folk. They are thorough and down-to-earth, their faces readable, their dreams practical. The men are part-time fishermen and partial summertime attractions in the enormous stormworn weatherboard pub William Dobell first painted and made famous: it looked like something a time warp had whisked away from eighteenth-century Cornwall. The women are perennial fencemongers rather than fishwives, and once they are nineteen become middle-aged overnight: as a lot of Australian country women do after they have learnt a man's cock is not the be-and-end-all of living.

"Children," Miss Cruikshank said, "Tuggeroo is the only valley town that will live for ever, thanks to Mr. Dobell's painting which will some day be recognized as one of the most memorable of man's inheritances. I will now ask you to make comments on this print I have, which is merely a silhouette of the majestic original hanging in the New South Wales Art Gallery."

"Miss Cruikshank? 'Silhouette'?"

"Not just now, Alice dear."

An old bridge of many-timbered teeth connects the fishing village with the outskirts of Kincomba, the hub of the shire, across the mud flats.

"What a stinkin' way to be connected."

"Old Tuggeroo Mac and his daughter built that bridge. Killed 'er, poor bitch!"

"He's still livin', but. Th'old bastard's ninety if he's a day . . . and still chasin' snatch."

"Aw, come off it!"

"I didn't say he could still come."

The truth is (and who's interested?) Tuggeroo Mac is alive, not-so-well, and living in ruptured bliss.

"Don't know why . . . his bloody daughter did all the hard yakka."

"She was a . . . hermophadite, ya know?"

"Oh fuck, grub! Don't start that again. The only hermaphrodite on the lake is Fisho Tatum's brig."

"I didn't know Fisho 'ad a daughter."

Kimcomba is the shire seat . . .

"Where all the big bums sit."

Most Kincomba citizens (Cucumbers) behaved in a city-like way, inspiring an enormous capacity to hate in the rest of the valley people. It was a well laid out, fair-sized country town run by a Council of nine men and one woman . . .

"Most of 'em too fat to even jog!"

These Councillors were intent on keeping the shire as safely out of the red as they could while enriching themselves without blackening their characters.

"An' their police only traffic in bribes."

"They reckon if ya live on a Councillor's street in Kincomba, you'll never have a rut in your road..."

"... or the rates in your pocket."

Even Miss Cruikshank was disinclined to argue with her classes about their Cucumber prejudices. They knew it and sometimes used it as a way to get her to glox on, which was not her normal bag.

"Why *does* everybody hate Kincomba, Miss Cruikshank? Are all cities like that?"

"Kincomba is hardly a city, Marjory. It is a burgeoning big town, and will some day be as big — and small time — as Newcastle and Wollongong. You have to look farther afield to find real people. Real people live right here in Boomeroo but *not* on our perimeters. Ungenerous (and childish) prejudices won't allow us to understand the nearby differences..."

Once or twice a year those little bastards had her in their power and she would forget the lesson at hand, and be unaware of their cunning.

"Who cares if the *Ceramic* and not the *Stratheden* called at Hobart once upon a time to take apples to England?

"... when you are older and travel — as I hope some of you shall — you'll realize the rest of the world is not so entirely different. Let me tell you about a trip I took when I went to Europe a few years ago.

"There's a train that leaves Venice at dawn. It goes to Vienna via Trieste. You soon realize that the people you meet on it could live on your street, wherever you live in the world. They smile with your eyes and they walk with your feet. Nothing is so different about them. You listen with their ears and... you try to speak with their hands. You recognize their neighbor's face. He lives next door to you, so you never feel too far from home.

"Those unending valleys are filled with the same ovation of nature you will find here. Little streams abound: they pour right out of heaven, peaceful and annealing . . . ask me about that later, Shirley.

"There are roads as intricate as the Tower of Babel, leading to mountain-top towns as magnetic as hope. The laughter of the people speaks of happiness and makes you wonder what you have done wrong with your own life.

"The children are filled with . . . the love in their days . . . soon you are living in their joyful world. By the time you arrive in Vienna you feel reborn, but . . . this new world you have discovered is really your own dear world, which you left in Venice at dawn."

Their silence was her reward.

Houses bob along the verdant south bank of Dooragul Creek, wandering off from Kincomba. Tracked together like floats on a fishing net they inevitably knot up in places. Like Winchester. A pretty spot on a cool shoal . . . too close to Kincomba stockyards, and much too close to a sad, stinking knackery owned by Councillor Duxmann.

"In summer you might as well sleep with ya nose up your wife's arse."

"In summer, if you lived in Winchester, you'd have a sore arse after all those Sydney poofters went back from their holidays."

Upstream, squatting beside the creek, is Nulla Nulla, nursed by a crippled rump of the Booradeela. In the Aborigines' Dreamtime, according to the carvings in the Mount Kaiser caves, this rump of the range sat in the water to put out a devastating bushfire. And so . . .

"Nulla Nulla was a sacred Abo spot once."

"Could be. Black Douglas still does his shaggin' on the tomato slopes. That crazy bastard fucks downhill, and leaves a bloody trail after him like as if forty fuckin' virgins had been lost in a cherry orgy."

24

Nevertheless, when the last full-blooded Aboriginal had gone beyond the face of that ugly mountain which his ancestors had simply called The Skull, the mystery of Nulla Nulla's splendid coign of vantage, the secret of its perfect tomato weather, remained unsolved.

The grade of the valley becomes more apparent between Nulla Nulla and Wollondonga, where it begins to taper. A billabong . . .

"Bloody swamp, you mean."

. . . known as Wollbung Bend keeps Wollondonga a precious distance apart from the knoll on the north side which makes Boomeroo more eminently situated. Wollondonga has become an infamous joke of a town because it's where the valley Sanitary Depot is. Kincomba is the only town sewered in the Lillipilli shire.

"If I was a shit-carter, every Christmas I'd go and dump a load in Cucumber Domain."

"You lazy cunt. If you was a shit-carter you wouldn't even carry Granny Green's piss-pot as far as 'er dunny."

Officially Wollondonga is a coal town and the mine there has one of the deepest shafts in Australia. The great wheel above the pit hauls up a rich if limited amount of blasted and hard-shovelled jet black coal.

"Hardly any coal dust down the Wolly . . . solid bloody coal!"

"And no gas. If I was a canary I'd be happy goin' down that shaft."

"If you was a fuckin' canary you'd be so yellow they'd deport you back to China."

There are several townships north of the creek, both north and east of Boomeroo, where the whipping pit whistles interrupt the miner's drinking and the disconsolate ring of the cowbells commands the lives of dairy farmers. The roosters shake the dawn.

"Don't need a watch. The chooks get you up an' Daisy's always five minutes early an' Strawberry's always six minutes late."

These are small communities where pubs determine the workload of the miners, fowls the life plan of the chicken farmers, and milking time the working hours of the dairies.

The original free-selections became populated crossroads, expanding — without the skerrick of a plan — to annihilate more and more of the bush. One township had been an old penal settlement. Still emerging into the twentieth century, caught between the advance of civilization and the retreat of the blacks, pioneers and misfits built fences where once escaped convicts had built bark huts.

The settlements were named after long-gone inhabitants, landmarks of some frail comedy or uproarious tragedy. Neaves Gully. Cattle-duffer Downs. Hudsons Run. Bruffs Stockade. Rhondda Gone. Stinking Biddy Springs. Fragile beginnings but cornerstones. And people still existed in these forsaken havens: in anger, friendliness, happiness, innocence, sadness and guilt, living in yesterday and today . . . but what of tomorrow?

"The trouble with those places, their pubs went phut." Three minutes' awe. "Once the pub goes there ain't a thing worth stayin' for."

"Take Minmi . . . ever been to Minmi?"

"The grub's Timbuctoo!"

"Fuck-all there except the pub."

"That's what I'm getting at if you'll zipper your teeth. Mine closed ages ago and no one gave a shattered shit. But you take away the Minmi pub an' what've you got?"

"Min-fuck-all!"

"That happened to Rhondda Gone. Mine closed and nobody gave a tinker's piss so long as you could still ride ya horse inta the bar. The pub went down the drip-tray . . . an' now Rhondda's really fuckin' Gone."

"Like Glen Davis."

"You gollion . . . you'll never learn. We're talking about . . . social misjustices! Don't you understand anything? Glen Davis was a 'normous political fuck-up. Billy Hughes woulda been proud of that one."

Apart from Boomeroo only three of these northside entrenchments could be called townships.

Chadla is an old timber town that almost expired with the bullock teams used to haul logs from the Booradeela Range before the railway sliced the valley more cleanly in halves than the creek had ever been able to do. The Chadla Timbercutters Bridge had straddled the Dooragul to give access to the hard-timbered slopes of the Booradeela; but the bullockies and their teams, and the local carters with their draught-horse drays, had no hope against a State railway. These primitive merchants lost the Booradeela Timber Reserve when it was snavelled up even before the Depression by the Kincomba Building Combine with a wheedled government contract.

"An' they still pay depressin' wages."

But Chadla, that little old bad town, had rebounded back to life with a thriving vengeance during World War II when an Army barracks was built there. It had tried to live up to a bestowed Gallic reputation ever since.

"Yeah, but I wish the Army'd move outa Chadla. I'm not mad about livin' close to the brass-arse militia."

"Those Chadla molls know their business, but."

"How would you know, Pinhead? You wouldn't know the front door from the back of a whorehouse or a woman."

"An' your prick's got more fingerprints on it than them FBI files."

Chadla may not be ennobled by the Army's presence, but it is enriched on Fridays because nobody's out of work there. The quid is stronger than the social structure. Fathers and sons are big spenders. Husbands are fast learners. Mothers are sometime-whores and whores were sometimes daughters . . .

". . . and Army wives are up for grabs!"

Bora Bora, the real mining center of the valley, is populated by the best drinkers.

"Bora pit has more seams than a ship's deck."

"They twist more'n a drunken sort's stockin's, too."

"Some of that Bora coal travels more underground than above."

To the men who work this coalmine faith is a shining amber thing with froth on it, and it flickers thousands of feet down, in the drift darknesses of the buckling Bora Bora and the seeping wastelands of its cockroach-infested tributaries. The amber goddess encourages their efforts to finish the shift and get back to the beloved pub where they can wedge gusty words while telling the world out there and one another how wrong it is and how right they are.

"I wouldn't work in the fuckin' sulphur shed at the cement works even if I hadda scrub floors like Missie Deeds and live on a bun an' an apple a day."

"You wouldn't work if you was Menzies' fuckin'ephew!"

"Only fools and pit ponies work."

"They reckon they're gonna open up a lot of those old seams again."

"Not the Pacific seam, but? They never did get them bodies outa there."

"So . . . they'll find a lot of bloody enormous cockerfuckin'-roaches wearin' pit boots and black singlets."

In shire reports extolling production in the Bora Bora mine it was the words "Kincomba Coal Commission" on the letterhead that drew the attention of the State Coal Board. And the Commission was rewarded by the NSW Government with a red brick Georgian Head Office in Kincomba.

"If those Cucumber poofters had to go down a mine

they'd shit before their pants dropped and the cage fell ten feet."

At MacDonald Township you can see the agony of convicts artistically enshrined in the sandstone barracks and prison, now bleached and reconverted . . .

". . . in 1899 . . ."

. . . homes for pensioners.

"The year the hurricane lamp came to Canberra."

Those convict years are still evident in the godless graves scattered around the town. But feel proud if you are descended from these men who were flogged at the triangles till blood filled their boots. They walked away from it . . . after two hundred lashes, bleeding in a way Jesus never knew. They waded back into the salt water to rake the shells to make the lime. There were times when they couldn't bear it any more and a few of the Irish killed a few of the English floggers and were sent to the worse hell of Norfolk Island. You'd never think such men could die.

Their guts bred and their courage spread and their disrespect for order survived. The very hopelessness of their existence made freedom holier than life. To have survived when death was a luxury, *that* was their wealth, their providence, their will and testament in perpetuity.

"They reckon you'll soon have to pay the Kincomba Tourist Bureau just to browse through MacDonald Township . . ."

". . . to fill your 'eart with this in*glorious* proof of your *glorious* criminal 'eritage! That's exactly what it said on this 'ere brochure."

"I tell you, Maxine," Mrs. Allsop said, "the day I have to pay to visit my Great-aunt Veronica in MacDonald you can lock me in the Kincomba Domain public toilet for a weekend without a penny in me purse."

Nevertheless, the pensioners anchored in MacDonald Township and the post-war newlyweds who fled there to build their compact Service Loan homes care only that their lawns remain green right down to the edge of the gentle lake.

In this way the valley extends itself to verge upon and surround . . . dadadadadadadadadah . . . Boomeroo.
"The grub's Utopia!"
And nowhere else does the whole shape of nature seem more married to men. The world less worldly. The sky more exhilarant. The sunlight more concentrated.
"You can do a lot with sandsoap, too."
The earth more attesting.
"More, man, more!"
The vagaries of life more human. Each to his own celebration.
"On a clear day you can see the fish in the lake."
"The fish are bloody lucky they can't see us."
Boomeroo sits cockily on its breast of the valley with a windscreen-wiper view that affects all Boomeroosters in the pits of their filled bellies. A postcard panorama that waits to ambush your sight on hazeless days.
"Make sure you don't fart and disturb the sulphur heap."
When the sun is high and all's well with one's world the lake simpers and the streets of far-off (thank Christ) Kincomba look a bit like the plaid pattern of the front veranda rug. On an utterly cloudless day, Inch Island, in the ankle of Wessouthern Bay, looks like a landy hole.
"Aw, come off it . . . we aren't that . . ."
" 'Gullible,' Miss Cruikshank?"
"Gullible Trabels," Terry Madison said, his angelic face beaming.
"Mister Madison," their aged teacher said, "you will either apologize to George Trabels this instant or write out one hundred times: 'I am not Swift.' "
"I'm pretty fast, but!"

"Add to that: 'Nor am I very clever.' "

"Miss Cruikshank," Ella Robinson said, "shouldn't he rather write out: 'I am neither Swift nor very clever'?"

"I apologize, Georgie, I apologize!" Terry jumped up and wound his head around like a pilgrim in a trance at Mecca with Satan up his arse, Jesus beckoning, and Mohammed somewhere out there in a sandstorm.

"You're being officious again, Ella," Miss Cruikshank said, trying not to smile at the Madison boy's antics. She loved the beautiful Madison child, as did every other old lady in town except Granny Green, who loved dogs and cockies but hated kids.

Swiftie Madison was born.

Boomeroosters don't envy the rich farmers who live on the far side of the Terribana Hills.

"Just like to marry their daughters."

Below the left shoulder of Mount Kaiser, across a cleft in the hills, a wide, winding pennon of the resplendent Upper Doorabana River explores the domain of extensive homesteads in the rain-blessed, rolling Jindaboolawaringoondigi district.

"Those Jindaboola farmers send their daughters to school in Switzerland, ya know."

"I guess that's as good a place as any to learnta milka cow."

If you drove through Boomeroo you would no doubt give thanks that the spread of civilization didn't depend on a housewife in a shabby nightie with a cold piece of toast and a butter knife in her hands, her fleshy breasts soliciting a side fence. But the hearts of Boomeroosters do not exist without solace and their minds are not immune to fantasy. They know that to live and not want is to die.

"If I'd've been born in America, Eunie," Mrs. Allsop confided (confided?) to a close crony, Eunice Corroner, a woman of disastrous proportions and myopic hopes, "I probably would've been discovered by one of those Hollywood talent scouts because I have such a good singing voice . . ."

True.

". . . and because I've got a nose like Joan Crawford and hair like Rita Hayworth . . ."

"And a'arse like Jessie the elephant."

". . . not to mention my mouth's got a sexy twist like Miriam Hopkins's. And look. See? I've got a lovely throat like Norma Shearer."

"Anyone got a lovely rope?"

To appreciate Boomeroo was to understand this proud kind of bastardry in a land where bastards are best.

The children are amorphous and still play hide-and-seek loudly with the same abandon as they secretly indulge in stinky-finger. They dig for worms more often than they search for words, and remember very little of what they are not interested in. They also watch falling stars in a sky that might well be unequalled from any other vantage point in the universe.

"They reckon there's people and things livin' out there in space."

"How many of the bastards, y'think?"

"Gotta be more'n there is in Sydney."

"Fuck me dead! Wonder we can't hear the racket from here."

4

The eight-day clock on the mantelpiece above the kitchen stove had lost interest in correct time but continued ticking because it had been a clock for over a hundred years. Grandad wound it every Sunday morning to keep it chiming.

Monte and his grandfather never depended on manufactured time; if visitors needed to know they could always check with the pigeon clock in Monte's room. It was an old-timer encased in heavy rosewood and it was accurate, even if it did chatter madly every time the kid put in a pigeon ring to register a bird home.

"It's got a ticky-tricky heart," Grandad said, "and one of these Saturday's it's going to have a coronary."

It worked honestly and well enough to satisfy the Club Headquarters of the Lillipilli Valley Racing Pigeon Federation in Chadla.

Grandad always had a cup of tea waiting for his grandson when he got home from school; it was one of the unchanging things in their way of life. Sometimes Bill Swanton, Grandad's oldest friend, shared this ritual; but lately Bill seemed hardly more than a tenant of his former robust self.

"Just suddenly got old," Grandad said. "Like as if he was tired of bein' young."

"You're never gonna get old, are you, Grandad?"

"I'm sure enough not going to give in overnight, Boy."

They didn't have an electric stove because Grandad argued he needed something to keep him occupied; and stacking the coal stove every few hours gave him that.

After Monte poked his freckled forehead into the kitchen to make sure Grandad was pottering with the teapot he went to his bedroom and changed into old clothes. He stuffed his school bag (an Army-issue gas-mask sack he traded a hundred marbles for) under his bed then went in to afternoon tea.

"Was my pigeon peas in the Co-op order today?" He poured his own cuppa.

"They were," Grandad said, then sipped from his ancient colonial teacup with the anti-moustache lip. He no longer had a moustache or beard.

"It looks like a shaving mug," Monte once said.

"The handle's on the opposite side to a shaving mug," Grandad replied.

The kid laced his tea liberally with condensed milk from a can with a creamy, hard-coated hole. Sometimes at night when Grandad pumped his own cup with rum he allowed the boy a smidgin.

Plonking himself at the table, the young pigeon-flyer said, "I think I'll buy a new scraper for the ducket . . . a long flat-ended one. I don't like that old triangle thing. I got thirty bob saved."

"You'll get one for less than a quid," Grandad said. "But you keep saving your money for High School next year; the Store Divvy will cover the cost of a new scraper."

"Bewdy!"

Boomeroo was a Co-operative Store town, and the Divvy was the most resilient type of money ever devised by man — and spent by woman. Dividends were paid twice a year, and winter clothes for kids and Christmas toys were only the beginning of its elasticity.

"I like to think of the Divvy the way Christ thought about the loaves and the little fishies," Mrs. Allsop said. "I was merely a girl in the Depression, Kate, and I probably wouldn't've ever had new bloomers if it hadn't been for the Divvy. Old Mumma got us girls new bloomers twice a year; milanese in summer and Viyella in winter. She'd say: 'You've got to have fresh bloomers every day even if no one sees them.'"

"Fresh duds every day maybe keeps crabs and cocks away."

Mrs. Allsop was indeed once a young girl. A flower in fresh bloomers, perhaps saved from a fate worse than fame by Amelia Bloomer and the Store Divvy.

Grandad swallowed a hot mouthful of tea and Monte sucked blackberry jam seeds from his teeth.

"You got the last youngun out today, son. Looks like you'll have some pretty good pigeons this year."

Monte slapped his cup down. "Great!" He blew up his tummy. He could do that: it was a disgusting habit.

"Rr-arrrh."

"Don't belch at the table," Grandad said, scraping his pipe. He tapped it delicately on the edge of the table so the ashes would fall in a cupped hand; then he flicked them across to the hearth. He was finicky about this and never blew his ashes every-which-way like Bill Swanton.

"For Godsake, Bill! Can't you be a bit tidy? There's food on the table."

His grandfather was every leaf of the family tree to Monte, and he dreaded the thought of losing him, and watched for signs of feebleness. But Grandad, who had only recently retired at sixty, was healthier than most men of fifty who lived less wisely. Monte knew the old man had to get older but he was sure (hoped fervently) it would be with . . .

"Miss Cruikshank? 'Dignity'?" One day during a lull between subjects he confronted his teacher.

" 'Dignity' is a noun of real worth," Cruikshank said. "It means a certain excellence. A stateliness, too. I think of it as something shining in a person which may not exactly glow but which is likely to shimmer in the beholder's eyes. Something a man or woman has that doesn't have to be proved. Yes . . . something innate." Kate Cruikshank was very interested in the sway of dignity.

Monte had decided that's how his grandfather would grow old: dignified, and of real worth.

Richard Montgomery Howard was irregularly freckled but without that pale yukkie complexion a lot of redheaded people have. His hair was already turning a dark mole-brown. With a low forehead and ears temple-high, he was sometimes called a throwback.

"That means an outcast," he complained.

"Oh . . . I wouldn't say that," Grandad said. "You look a lot like me. 'Cept your bloody nose, of course."

Monte's nose was lumpy where a cricket ball had broken it.

"A real six-stitcher too, Mr. Delarue."

"You doan say! How abart that?" The Boomeroo Yank was puzzled. "Can't see a trace of any stitches there, kiddo."

"The ball was a six-stitcher not me busted nose," Monte explained patiently.

Tony Delarue looked lost somewhere between baseball and the rites of spring. The American had spent six months hunting kangaroos and emus before he established the town's laundrette; and though he often teased the kids about the emptiness of their country and the drivel of their customs they never stopped asking him to settle their arguments. He was the ultimate authority on America.

"Seems crazy to play a sport where you can get a busted nose without a fight or a hassle."

"I was fielding silly-mid-off, but."

"That sounds a bit like Jesse James complaining the posse had bullets in their guns," Tony said, licking a grin across his lips. America to him was gone, and then some, and he didn't understand all the local interest in it. When he took that subject up with his wife, Nance, she said, "It's the Hollywood syndrome. We grew up on Sunset Boulevard."

Monte's mouth was too evident considering the smallness of his chin. His face was fatter than a full moon, but his body skinny, and his arms hung almost to his knees.

"You got arms like a monkey," Duck Allsop said too gamely and was half throttled to death by a chimpanzee limb.

"Your hair's a bit porcupiney," Swiftie said, scratching his cock. "You're lucky it ain't round your balls."

"Say your tuppence-worth and get it over with before you cop a bellyful of knee," Monte said, grinding teeth Bela Lugosi would have been proud of.

"Ain't as bad as bein' like Granfarver Jones," Batter said in a placating manner, "an' havin' eyes like two bubbles in a piss-pot."

"And people don't throw up when they look at you, even if you are a throwback," Gloamy said, jumping out of the way of a flung foot.

Monte Howard had been the first boy — in boy memory that is — to paddle a canoe to Tuggeroo and back. It took him till long after dark and half the kids in town were out hopefully looking for fame by finding his upturned canoe and bloated body.

He was the youngest whippersnapper who ever dived —

not jumped — from the top frame of the Highway Bridge into the creek. And guess who invented the notorious pastime of shitting in Bora Bora two-up forum when you were in that vicinity of the Terribana Hills? First boy (well, first in a hell of a long time) to swim underwater from bank to bank of Dooragul Creek. He was called Mullet for months afterwards.

He was very proud of being the youngest-ever paid-up member of the Lillipilli Valley Racing Pigeon Federation Club. *That* was important.

Monte's Mum died when he was born and his Dad was killed at Tobruk.

"A dead rat," Duck Allsop said and got symbolically thrashed for that one.

Mrs. Allsop insinuated that his mother may never have been married. "In any case, June, nobody could be positive that Boy Howard was the father. Katey Singleton was a flighty young thing."

Monte had heard that rumor himself through the saloon bar window one Saturday afternoon when the gang was hanging round the pub hoping to earn a thrippence or two running bets to the SP bookmaker at the billiard room. It hadn't hurt his heart and barely singed his pride. Grandad said that Bill Howard was his father and Grandad didn't lie. It was as simple as that.

" 'He drinks and he swears, and he fights at times, and his name is mostly Bill . . .' Henry Lawson wrote that, didn'e?"

This kid did know for a positive fact that somewhere in his throat was a knot connected to a lump in his stomach between which raced hundreds of fronded feelings . . . all to do with Grandad. Feelings that flickered electrically like the sky-ceiling of the giant Capital theater in Sydney where Grandad and he had filled in a few hours waiting for a train.

His grandfather often had a few days' growth on his face; but when he was clean-shaven his features were retrievably Monte's. Except for the freckles. They were loners at heart but identifiably related, in heart and mind as well as in blood.

"I won't go to the matinee to see *The Corsican Brothers* if you wanta take me tonight, Grandad."

"Oh, you go along. I saw his [Douglas Fairbanks Junior's] Dad in the silent."

"OK. But remember you *are* comin' to see *Red River* with me when it comes back."

"All right! I still don't expect it to be better than *The Big Trail*."

At breakfast they often discussed the gall of the British Empire. From Khyber to Gallipoli, through the Crimea and the Boxer Rebellion to the Boer War. The Relief of Mafeking invariably meant burnt toast.

"The British sure got around, didn't they? They didn't sit on their bums like the United Nations."

"Just because the earth turns doesn't mean you can run it from a swivel chair, Boy."

"Clive of India sure got off his arse!"

"Don't get carried away . . . you got a few years to go before you can throw *your* pens and pencils out the window."

Lunch could be a historical smorgasbord. Baked beans and the Spanish Civil War. Tinned spaghetti was appropriate to the Italians in Abyssinia.

Cheese sandwiches and the War of American Independence. Hamburgers and the American Civil War.

"Mr. Delarue calls the American Civil War the War between the States."

"That's his prerogative."

"You got some good words up your sleeve, Grandad."

"And you haven't got much time up yours before the schoolbell rings."

Grandad had the education of time behind him and could afford illusions for two. Monte liked to sew things up as easily as an appendix operation.

The Russo-Japanese War was a sticky wicket.

"That Jack London's a great writer, but."

"Not a very good reporter, though. He never seemed to have a good grasp on the real issue of that conflict."

"Does it matter now, Grandad?"

"When the past doesn't matter you won't have much future worth worrying about . . . Boy!"

Monte loved teatime. You could linger into the night digesting a poet or two. Lawson. Banjo Paterson. Other early Australians who took their axes and pens, swags and paper, horses and hopes, raging hearts and wit-leavened heads into the unpromising bush to anatomize and reconstruct its un-English dissonance. Monte liked the poem about a bushranger named Jack Dean: "Taking His Chance." Jack Dean's girlfriend wasn't like the sheila in *Red River*; she was never in the way.

"May Carney would never cop an arrow in the tits."

May Carney understood that Jack Dean had his bushranging to do and just wanted to be waiting for him whenever he had time for a dance . . . and, of course, when he died. Monte loved the awesomeness of a dying bushranger with the guts to turn to his girl rather than make peace with God on his last breath. It was a frightening . . . conjecture. That was one of Grandad's.

"Women are different, aren't they?"

"When they want to be," Grandad said. "But you start treating them different and you're in the oven. Of course, they get used to you being indifferent. There's a difference!"

"Cor . . . Grandad, I'll never understand them."

"Well, you won't be alone in this country."

Some nights they listened to radio serials and sometimes they read. Dickens, Scott, Stevenson, Hawthorne, George

Eliot: these were the bricks in Grandad's bookcases. And they each had a favorite book that came from America. Grandad's was *Moby Dick*. Monte's was the dog-eared, nail-scratched and much-read copy of *The Red Badge of Courage*. Stephen Crane's *boy* was his closest acquaintance in fiction.

Some nights they were just plain bloody grouchy and niggled each other.

"Cook may have been the world's greatest navigator ever, but he died stupidly," Grandad said.

"But he was an adventurer and did what he wanted to do. Miss Cruikshank says that's important: how you live . . . not just what you leave for people to bicker over."

"Oh, so now I'm bickering?"

"No, Grandad! I didn't mean that. I can't exactly explain . . . *exactly* what I mean."

"Sorry if I flamboggled you, but repeating yourself won't help."

"You're an old bugger at times!"

"Watch it, Boy, or you're gonna get the hidin' of a lifetime."

The best nights were when Grandad's old pit cronies came round and relived the lives of those most bereaved persons who ever lived to die: the Australian bushrangers. And, oh God, how they died! How often they all died. Monte related to Johnnie Gilbert (even if he was a flash cove) because he chose to bushrange and never blamed anybody for driving him to it.

"Not like the bloody Kellys. They had more excuses than a whore with syphilis every time they fucked up."

Johnnie Gilbert died game so his mate, Dunn, could escape. You'd get to Ben Hall's heaven on that one! Too bad he had been born in Canada.

"Ben Hall had twenty-seven bullets in him."

And a thousand fanatic admirers for every ounce of lead.

4 1

"They caught Thunderbolt in the mud and butchered him. The cunts cut him to pieces."

All troopers were cunts.

Thunderbolt. The local evocation. How often had he galloped the length of the Lillipilli Valley?

Not so often.

"Wiff a laugh in front of him and the troopers behind." Granfarver Jones always said that. You could toss two pennies on it. Sometimes with a wiff and sometimes wiff-out.

"Granfarver Jones once had a drink with him in the old Tuggeroo pub."

"Even called him Fred."

"Tell about it, Granfarver. Tell about the time Thunderbolt robbed the Bank of New South Wales in Kincomba, swam his horse across the creek and stopped at the Tuggeroo pub for a noggin . . ."

". . . just to give the troopers time to nelly catch up."

And the old drunk bag-belly will tell it again. You can bet your pit pony's balls on it.

If it was a beer-cold night after a smoking hot day, and if there happened to be a few young blades there drinking, building up bravery to visit the whorehouse next door, everyone got carried away.

"It was better in them days. It was sorta like . . . Sydney or the bush."

"Preferrin' to live like a man in the Weddin' Mountains to bein' flogged like a cunt at Bathurst or Castle Hill."

If the word "bastard" meant love by strange rebuttal then "cunt" was the most derogatory word ever applied to man, its true meaning ignored.

Later, Jerry Kyle would be encouraged to sing, the chastity of his sweet soprano feeding their sentimentality and bringing tears even to Bill Swanton's beer-aged eyes.

"I've been a prisoner at Port Macquarie,
At Norfolk Island and at Emu Plains;
MacDonald Township and Too . . . oongabbie;
At all those settlements I've worked in chains.
But of all those places of condemnation
And penal stations in New South Wales,
To Moreton Bay I have found no equal;
Excessive tyranny each day prevails.

"Like the Egyptians and Ancient Hebrews
We were oppressed under Logan's yoke . . .

". . . and when from bondage we are liberated
Our former suffering shall fade from mind."

After these nights there were dreams and often nightmares. Convict transports. Hungry, crowded, sail-proud and beautiful from a distance, bellying through purling seas. Heavy-gutted with highwaymen, murderers, pimps, pickpockets and poachers, bread-thieves and strumpets, bony boys and giddy little girls who may have stolen a gentleman's silk handkerchief. Men and women who lacked everything and had the audacity to live for one more day . . . and then another.

"Mary Reiby was thirteen when she was transported for takin' a ride on someone's horse."

"Christ! Wish we could get Duck Allsop sent up for that. You leave ya bloody horse tied up outside one pub then find it outside another. Then yer missus goes crook and reckons you're too drunk to remember where you were drinking."

Lags escaping from Pinchgut Island in Sydney Harbor. Living with the Aborigines. Being cannibal. Starving to death in the brooding gashes of Jamieson Valley. Holing in and holding out in that sanctuary of the bushranger, The Hollow. Floods sweeping down the Wollondilly, wrapping up pioneers, their possessions and their hopes, in a wilderness of water.

"When Granny Green was a girl . . ."

". . . they launched the Ark."

". . . things once got so bad they made porridge outa the fowl pollard . . . after they'd ate the chooks."

"Leslies trace one side of their family back to the First Fleet."

"How lucky can you get? That was like a Sunday trip to Taronga Zoo compared to the Second Fleet. What was left of those poor bastards crawled ashore."

"Of course, things *were* grim in England."

"Things are always bloody grim in England, ya nitshit."

"*Lecherous whoremasters who practice vile arts,
To ruin young virgins and break parents' hearts,
Or from the fond husband the wife lead astray,
Send such debauched stallions to Botany Bay.*"

"Sounds like Mt. Isa."

"Nowhere's like Mt. Isa. Livin' in Stinking Biddy Springs beats livin' there."

"Grandad? I'm not sure why those two kids jumped off the cliff in *For the Term of His Natural Life*."

"There are some things worse than the end, Richard." That "Richard" meant: Ask me again in a few years' time.

Vividly summing up her views on the nation's frightful beginnings, Mrs. Allsop said, "Look at it this way, Hilda. If the Poms hadn't sent someone here that French fella, Larpa Roos, would have claimed the place for France . . . an' we'd all be eating snails and frogs' legs. How'd you like that gup instead of plum pudding for Christmas?"

It was hard to find someone without a fling of pride in his ancestors. Monte was descended from convicts through Grandad, whose full name was Richard Aaron Brough Singleton. The kid was probably prouder of being descended from the rough Broughs than from the genteel Martha Singleton and the celebrated Captain Singleton.

On his Grandma Howard's side, Richard Montgomery

was, not so proudly, treed to Granfarver Jones who claimed every lag from Wales in the First, Second and Third Fleets among his forbears.

"What kinda name is *Aaron*?" Duck said. "Hair-on what? His Richardy-dick?" And got a fast foot up his slow arse.

"In the Bible, Aaron had a *rod*," Gloamy said, then added after a snarly look from Monte, ". . . don't mean he had a horn all the time."

It was nice to know where you came from. Monte felt sorry for people who knew nothing more than a vast, vague shadow beyond their grandparents' past.

Laying his pipe aside, Grandad said, "Red-checker ain't going to be a very good mother. She's on and off the nest all day hankerin' to get through the wire to the blue-bar cock. I'd move her if I was you."

Sitting with one leg crossed horizontally beneath the other, Monte said, "Goodio. I'll put her in the bottom ducket where I've got it whitewashed ready for the squeakers." He jumped up as if ant-bitten. "I better scoot! They'll be dyin' to get up for their fly."

Wetting his lips, he bundled his body out the back door and, whistling, ambled down to the pigeon ducket. Twenty-seven birds recognized that whistle and their gurgling response brought him an uplifting satisfaction. It was natural to try all the shots at the carnival when it hit town, but you had to have something to fill the cavities when the time for clowning came to an end.

Thinking of Johnnie Gilbert he walked like John Wayne.

> . . . *Gilbert walked from the open door*
> *in a confident style and rash* . . .
>
> . . . *and he turned to his comrade, Dunn:*
> *"I'll stop and fight with the pistol here . . ."*

"*Pow-pow-pow* . . ." Monte drew and slaughtered the besiegers.

The pigeons did not reel; they were used to these boyish histrionics. Moving in almost erotic precision, they flicked their heads this way and that like people at a Wimbledon Final who haven't relieved their bladders for hours.

He propped open a wire panel and the birds took to the sky in a riot of wings.

"Give my love to Mrs. Kafoots," he called after them. Everybody knew about Mrs. Kafoots . . . only nobody knew where she came from or where she lived.

5

ALTHOUGH ITS EDDYING population is quiet, Boomeroo is not stagnant. Imaginations are running and plans are coined if not always minted. A few ideas are fresh, and some souls are regularly thirsty. Feelings clutch you and discover that particular *you* indigenous to your nature.

Boomeroo is where the North-West Railway and the Great North-West Highway split. The tracks stay south of the creek and nose under the Booradeela through the Frisco tunnel which had its unexpected beginnings in the San Francisco Mine — the effort and dream of a long-gone Yankee goldminer called Radley, who was a runner, a foot-racer in those days when man challenged man with his own fleet body.

The highway crosses Dooragul Creek, barges through Boomeroo and tackles the sudden and prospective rise through Oxford Pass. It provides Boomeroo with the only decent bridge across the Dooragul.

All the trains except the Brisbane Express stop here on their way between Kincomba and Walla Walla, a grazing center nearly a hundred miles the other side of the mountains. The spirit of Boomeroo is as unbroken as a brumby, and common stubbornness as binding as the cement manufactured in the town's economical mainstay.

A welcome sign tells you that Boomeroo is . . . A GOOD REXONA TOWN. But, let's face it, nothing shattering has happened here since Angela Withers (the Ten-bob Angel) was caught in Mr. Garrison's bed when she was fourteen.

"*Waylaid*, really. By Mrs. Garrison hidin' under the bed."

"That's what I call waiting for fate on the banks of the Po, Renee."

"An' don't forget Bert Hinkler crashed on the old racecourse between here and Chadla!"

"Bert Who?"

"Hinkler Who, that's who, you ignorant fuckin' grub. Just the greatest flier ever. He coulda flew shit outa Kingsford-Smith and Lindbergh even if they'd shoved propellers up their arses."

"Hey! They've got Billie Hawke in jail again."

"What for this time?"

"Not havin' feathers up his bum like other birds."

A legendary gambler called Dud Penny won a fortune the year Flight *didn't* win the Melbourne Cup and bought the freehold of the biggest pub in Kincomba. This is important because Boomeroosters still get their first beer free in Penny's Pub.

Dud Penny is a hero but the game little mare, Flight, is as near to sainthood as any animal might hope for.

"Gamer than Simpson's donkey!"

These pubbling people put shameless value on incidentals, yet their incidental awareness of true value is far more real than their loud disgusts.

"A National Uranium mob is buggerin' round just the other side of Oxford Pass."

"We'd go ahead like Rum Jungle if they found that stuff here."

"I'd just'soon the town grew natural-like."
"That'd be slow-friggin' growin'!"
"Ah . . . twenty–thirty years'll see us on our way."
"That's a bloody long time to frig."
"Be worse if we sold our soul like Broken-bloody-Hill."
"So . . . how we know you haven't sold your own arsehole in Mt. Isa?"

The sun rises and the moon dwindles when the man on the wireless says so . . . predict, he doesn't. The Southern Cross is an opulent luxury you can afford to ignore in such a monstrously stunning sky. You live enveloped by an ocean of stars, some of which on a clear night feel like diamonds in your uplifted hands. Good advice from friends or enemies can be as practical and cruel as abuse can at times be beautiful.

"Listen, buddy, I know you're an American an' you mean well . . . but, if you don't put in for the fuckin' Anzac wreath this year people are gonna think you're a cunt'ooks."

"Next time you clock your missus, draw the bloody curtains before you do, you stupid shit."

"Look, bastard-face, if you don't keep away from my sheila I'll belt Christ outa *her* face till she looks like a hatful of maggots. Then you can 'ave 'er . . . but you won't be no mate of mine."

Australia is a country of Aspirinauts and Boomeroo is no exception. To be told to take a powder doesn't mean: Get lost!

"If you've got a pain take a bloody Bex but don't come bellyachin' to me."

Never argue about indisputable facts everyone from five to five-score knows . . . such as this: Jack Lang was the best fuckin' Labor Leader we ever had.

"He was a bloody white man and that makes him a bloody . . ."

"... unique politician."

"Listen Rosie, I'd still be voting for Jack Lang if he wasn't dead."

Why bother to tell her that he's alive and well and living in the past. Politically, you can brag about one Party one day and moan about it the next so long as you . . .

". . . vote Labor on election day."

God may be no more evident than in the brown, unsmiling weatherboard vestibule of the Church of England church or the Catholic church's tired brick facade, but this does not mean He is not around and partly appreciated.

"The Sallies see to that."

God is established, if not evident, in the good where He belongs, in the bad where He is needed, and in the indifferent where least suspected.

"What about *real* sinners, but?"

"You mean those adulterous, deviate, cloven monsters who fuck for fucking's sake anything with hair, skin, fur or feathers between its legs?"

"Bejesus . . . yeah!"

"They've all gone to Sydney."

"I'm a wicked woman, Ida. You know at Mass sometimes I get this awful joyful . . . unredeemed urge to stick my head under his cloth and see how big it is."

"Me? I'd like to grab his hot holy hands and press them to me crotch."

In spite of the sulphur fumes from the cement works, the only things that suffocate are the damp chicken feathers in Mrs. Allsop's house-made cushions.

"She makes them for the Catholic raffles, but they make sure the Protestants win 'em."

"Things *are* different Down Under."

"Yeah . . . 'snot our fault if the bloody May bush blooms in September."

"And where else does a pre-fuckin' bride carry bloody November lilies?"

They live in an old weatherboard . . .
". . . ramshackle . . ."
. . . place next to Vonnie Kyle's big white house on Harrow Street. That's how locals would direct you to the dull, flowerpot-ochre cottage built by Grandad in 1912 before the twentieth century began to rumble.

Some of their out-of-town pigeon-flying friends never knew that the popularly known building next door was a heaven on earth (compared to Big Fat Nellie's shack) for all the wise young men and old foolish devils on the Northside who didn't fancy paying for a high time with the worldly short-time Army whores of Chadla's abounding brothels.

"You can't fuck the Ten-bob Angel for less than a quid any more, but."

"You can still screw Nellie for a hot meat pie any time of the day or dark."

"I'd rather fuck the hot kidney pie!"

"I like Feet-Feet. She makes you feel good. Like as if she's enjoyin' it too when you sink your cock into 'er."

"The best Chadla molls charge ten quid."

"An' some of their twats feel like buckram!"

"They suck it for you first, sometimes."

"That's fuckin' inflation."

"No . . . that's inflated fuckin' . . . they make you wear a Frenchie."

"Well . . . I still think Feet-Feet's best. An' sometimes, if she ain't busy, she comes with ya!"

The Singleton house had only the essential rooms. The front bedroom was Grandad's. It was choked with an enormous Chippendale suite worth more than the house and land. Monte had the side bedroom. It was stacked with cheap pine furniture made by his Uncle Mitch (his mother's twin) killed in the same German push on Tobruk as Bill Howard.

"We shoulda had Rommel on our side."

Rommel, like Ben Hall, was above nationalities, politics and law. No prize for betting your desert boots on that. All the young men who had died in World War II were now enshrined in the enormous frame in the School of Arts with photos of their fathers and uncles and grandfathers who had died in the Great War.

Also, one of the concrete faces of the underpass beneath the Highway Bridge had become a rough memorial wall, kept strangely clean of the usual graffiti. A guy called Nickie Johnson went on the piss on VP Day with half a gallon of wompy, a toothbrush and a small tin of red paint, and plastered his mourning on a high cheek of the concrete ramp where it still recalled:

> In memory of my mate Chidley-didley
> Howard who died at Tobruk DAMN.

"He's a boss at the cement works now."

"Ain't 'e your godfather, Monte?"

"Yep. Every year on me birthday he gives me a quid. Grandad said that when I was a baby and had this Pinks disease, Mr. Johnson used to come down early every morning and take me for a long walk in the pram."

"Gee . . . him and your Dad musta been real mates."

"Yeah!"

Others, deprived of more than they ever officially complained about, enlisted friends' and relatives' names on the concrete to ease their unanalyzed tears.

> Biddy Waverley EL ALAMEIN
> Eddie Mills lost over LILLE
> Hoddie Stevens THE KOKODA
> Even-Stevens CHANGI
> Billy Latter GREECE

Kipp Duncan was my Dad and the Japs killed him at Lababia Ridge. Peter James Kerr and Daniel Christopher Kerr died in Libya.
REMEMBER GOOD OLD SCREWDRIVER SIDNEY (EMDEN) FARREL WAS ONLY 16

In a white heart of curlicues someone had declared undying love for the missing-in-action Vincie Johnson.

"Vince Johnson took more maidens than any two famous cricket bowlers . . . ever!"

Monte often varnished his Uncle Mitch's furniture but never completely finished it as a single project; it had become a fretted exhibition of over-meeting shades. The kitchen was the common stomping ground, the washhouse a storeroom, and the living room was lined with ceiling-high oak bookcases.

Monte didn't hate water, just preferred it fresh and went swimming all year, if only once a week through July and August.

"Crikey, the creek was cold today, Grandad."

"Least there'd be no water snakes around."

"Heck, I didn't even run into one all last summer. I figure the puke from the cement works must be killin' 'em off."

"Sooner or later all that gup will get through Tuggeroo Wash into the lake, and *then* they'll haveta do something."

Words that Duck sang when there was a bunch of kids down the creek made sense to Monte. Duck would daub mud on his face, jig madly, whoop it up, and whale into "Old Black Alice."

> *"Old Black Alice are my name,*
> *Walla is my station;*
> *It's no disgrace this old black face,*
> *It's the color of my nation.*
> *White man wash in an old tin tub,*

Black man wash much cleaner;
Black man wash in the Condamine
Or in the Diamantina.
Dance with the black girl, whoop-de-do,
None of your money buys 'er:
Got a nice boy in Boomeroo
And another one in Mt. Isa."

Bill Swanton's willing old wife still came once a week to do the housework and laundry, and to leave a heated clean copperful of water for Grandad's bath. On the first day of the month they both pitched in and did the overdue accumulated chores.

"That's what Mr. Delarue calls odd jobs."

The first of the month was also Rabbit Day. "You get outa bed and run round the house three times yelling: 'Rabbit-rabbit-rabbit!' It brings ya luck."

"I did that once and got the mumps," Duck said.

"Orr . . . you couldn't piddle downhill if ya drank a gallon of lolly-water at the top of Ziggedy Ridge."

It was a man's house and everyone knows a man doesn't need the frills that fill a woman. If Grandma hadn't died fairly young, no doubt it would have been decorated several times and added to during pregnancies.

"I'll be alone in the world when you go, Grandad."

"I'm not *going* anywhere yet, Boy, not even to reap my acre. Besides, if you keep this house and its memories you'll never be alone. And I promise not to . . . go, till you marry and have kids — if you promise not to get married too young."

"An' I promise not to marry too young if you live till I make a fortune and can afford a better car than Mr. Leslie's."

"You mean I gotta live till they make a better car than a Rolls Royce?"

The boy's laughter bubbled and he grinned like a sinkhole. "You got the drift... you're quick on the uptake today, old man. Grandad? Maybe if I hadn't been born my Mum would still be here to look after you."

"Never think of it that way." He shook his head and closed his eyes momentarily. When he opened them and found his grandson probing him he smiled and engulfed the child in love.

"Poor Mr. Singleton. Losing the twins within a year of each other musta murdered 'im."

Mitch had been a gentle boy: a fund of intelligence. Katharine a golden wild and rampant girl, as recalcitrant as Eve, but brilliant. Her brain, merely brushed by education, awed her teachers.

"I heard Mrs. Allsop talking about Mum one day, Grandad, and she said something about dogs that chase cars finally get hit by a lorry. What did she mean *exactly*?"

"That some day *she's* going to get hit by a dirty big truck."

The pigeon ducket was Monte's retreat, and when necessary his sanctuary. Apart from school, cowboy pictures and some notorious escapades with his gang, Grandad and pigeons were the roughage of his life. Reality in bulk. The bond between him and his grandfather did not have to be guarded: it was absolute.

"Why couldn't Becky Sharp be more like Katharine Hepburn in *Quality Street* or Greer Garson in *Pride and Prejudice*?"

"You can't judge Thackeray by the old movies you see with your class at the School of Arts once a month."

It wasn't always easy for the old man. The boy had his moments, ranging from baby to devil to saint to little bastard. He could be jealous, fanatic, impatient, endearing. He represented all those whistle-stops of boyhood on the way to that ultimate state of manhood. Grandad was as patient and warm as the womb. His common sense was authentic and his basic intelligence innate.

"That Howard kid is a smart-arse little bugger!"
"But, by God, does he adore that old fella."
"Why not? Grandad Singleton'd give you his arse and shit through his ribs."
They loved each other in certain and no uncertain terms, with qualms to match everything except doubt.
"Grandad. Hey, Grandad, I got arms like Les Darcy."
"But you fight like a wrestler ... and since when was I goin' deaf?"
"I can lick most of the kids my age."
"They must be lousy fighters."
"Half a mo, old man!"
"Look, son, you've gotta learn to stand off and size up your opponent. Wham-bam-grapple isn't fighting."
"But if you win? Don't you think, considering ... ?"
When they reached that don't-you-think-considering stage even the pigeon clock stopped being liable for time. For a few realizing seconds you could hear a fly fart, then it was on ... another great Australian (almost unending) argument.
Almost!
"Well ... that's a matter for a referee. I still love ya, you old bastard."
"If that's dessert, you little bummer, I'd rather have apple dumpling. Now, how about bed?"
"How about a toddy? Me sheets'll be cold tonight."
"You make the tea, I'll stake the rum."
"I guess I was born lucky bein' dumped on you, Grandad. What do you reckon?"
"You want the truth or hot shit in a cup of Ovaltine, Boy?"
"I got the shoulders if you've got the message, *Mister* Singleton."
"As a matter of fact I had luckier days before I heard your cheeky little bum being smacked."
"Orr ... Grandad?"

6

Monte spent the short winter afternoons, Indian spring mornings, autumn dusks, long summer nights and other seasonal confections in his pigeon ducket. It was his brace and his bind and happiness engrossed him there. On his ninth birthday, when there was a mist hanging on the peg of the morning, a daggering sunstream had beamed through the wire and fell on a few favorite birds, and what until then had been a game became a dedication.

This castle of wire, conduit channels, concealed springs, butter-box walls, sapling standards and corrugated iron — pinched from the old racecourse fence . . .

"There isn't a kid on the creek without a canoe battered out of that inexhaustible supply of corrugated iron."

. . . was a lofty design of sliding panels, elevating doors, friendly traps for pigeons and frustrating barriers for inquisitive kids. His mates knew where to find him, but he wasn't easy to get at. Only Jerry knew of a secret entrance camouflaged into Kyle's fence . . . an escape hatch. Liking Jerry did not mean you understood him, but he made sense and asked appreciable questions. That mattered. Batter and Gloamy asked questions almost as annoying as Duck's.

"What's that one tumbling for?"

"Because he's a tumbler. He trapped in one day and I let him stay. Sorta as a mascot."

Swiftie was not interested in pigeons. Just girls. "You know Monique Johnson? Your godfather's daughter? She's got bulgy tits already. I'd sure like to tickle her tap." A clitoris was what Swiftie called a tap: it could have been a simile Miss Cruikshank would have understood.

The day they eventually discovered what it was really called in Mrs. Kyle's huge medical dictionary, Feet-Feet Anderson caught them and asked, "Why di'n't you come to me? I would've shown you. Come inta my room and I will!"

Monte and Jerry nicked off but Swiftie hung in there and had a good look. He reported: "It *was* a bit like a little red-hot tap. It reminded me of a drake's dick, too," And he knew. Once he had let a drake in with his mother's chickens and it really got stuck into them. A few were unhinged for weeks. Swiftie waited anxiously but none of them ever laid a duck's egg.

"And you know all about ducks and chooks," Monte said, wildly jealous.

"You're just mad 'cause mine's growin' faster than yours," Swiftie said.

"Arrh . . . piss off!"

"Don't worry, mate. Yours'll start growin' suddenly one day like mine did."

"Worry about your balls," Monte said. "They don't seem to be hangin' as good as mine. You told me y'self they disappear when you come."

"Yeah, that's amazing, ain't it?" Swiftie said, unperturbed. "Must be something that happens to us oversexed bastards."

If Duck Allsop saw a cock courting he would copy it, mumbling, "I'll-wop-it-up-you-I'll-wop-it-up-you."

"Get lost, Duck! Go flip your dirty big black retriever off." Duck did that sometimes.

Jerry noticed important things.

"That mealy hen's picking the mosaic-pied cock's toes."

"Damn! Grandad *never* had a toe-picker, so it can't be the breeding."

"It isn't natural in homing pigeons," Grandad said. "Tailpickers maybe . . . but toe-pickers? I don't know! But if dogs can go insane the same as men can . . . who knows? Pity. She's a good bird."

"Mr. Watson mixes eucalyptus oil and black shoe polish to dab on the toe-pickers among his chickens," Jerry said. "He says that takes the urge out of them but it seemed to me they got drunk."

"Wow!" They laughed companionably.

"What's the farthest you've flown, Mont?"

"Nearly six hundred miles. My best cock bird did that in less than eleven hours last year. They liberated him at five o'clock in the morning in Queensland and he was home here before four o'clock in the arvo."

"That's a long way. That's fast!"

"Birds fly straighter than roads, but."

"Zoweee!" Monte had never heard anybody but Jerry say that. "How come you call the younguns squeakers and Grandad calls them squabs?"

"Depends a bit on their age. But then how come people call the Bora two-up school a swy school now?"

"It's funny that, isn't it?" Jerry squinted. "The way things change. I read in this book of Angela's there mightn't even be a God. It read: 'Is God dying or already extinct?'"

"Like the American passenger pigeons," Monte said with authority. "There used to be so many of them they could cloud a sky for days. But who wants there not to be a God? He's handy at times."

"What makes a pigeon come home?"

"Eye-sign maybe. Sound? They say if you cover a pigeon's ears it flies at . . . random. I just reckon, well, they are homing pigeons, aren't they? That's their bag! They come home. Like us going to school. We have to bloody go. Bees and ants go home at night. Even stupid cows come home to be milked. Only thing I ever heard about that don't come home is . . . are girls."

"That's right," Jerry said. "Feet-Feet and Angela never go back home. And Maggie Gordon's sister, Callie, went to Kincomba for the weekend, an' next thing they get is a quick letter from Sydney saying she was leavin' on a ship that day to go to London. She did write a long letter from London to Miss Cruikshank, but, telling her she was going to Vienna. Feet-Feet talks about her mother a lot but Angela's very bitter . . . she'll never go home in a million years." Jerry was fascinated by the brittle and aloof Tenbob Angel. "Angela reads these intelligent books. I mean real intelligent books. Know what I mean?"

"No, and I don't care." Monte preferred the kind, candycrazy, walloping Feet-Feet to the Angel. If you were broke and it was a stinking hot day Feet-Feet would shout you a soft drink and chewing gum. And she was the one to keep Duck in line. No mucking around there. She'd clip Duck over the ears and call him a big-mouth fart like his mother. If he got too cheeky she'd dong him across the shoulders with one of her huge shoes which she never seemed to have on her feet but always in her hands. Smelly she might be, but Feet-Feet was as generous as honeysuckle on a warm night.

Like the afternoon she was trying on a new pair of shoes in front of a host of kids who were rollicking around Kyle's big back lawn. Duck said, "If ya can't get ya feet into them shoes the box they come in might fit ya." He got a hard strong big toe in the balls for that flippant suggestion and hopped home screaming, his hands between his legs and his knees in aspic.

"One night," Jerry said, "when Mum was in Kincomba, Mr. Rowlandson tried to get into bed with me and Angela belted hell out of him with the broom handle. She called him a bisexual old bugger," Jerry added with a sad inflection.

"I'll get you for this, you two-bob whore," Mr. Rowlandson shouted.

"You'll get nobody for anything and fuck-all from everybody if I broadcast it," Angela said, swiping him again with the broom handle while he was struggling back into his pants. "And if you come back here I'll stuff that black brolly of yours up your arse and open it wide."

"You mustn't get any sleep some nights," Monte said.

"You get used to voices," Jerry said. "They get to be humdrum and sometimes they help you doze off. But Mum's promised we'll move to Sydney if I want to go to University. Leave this town. You know how people talk."

"Well, if you hear Duck spruikin' I got something on him will shut him up," Monte said.

Monte had been present at the back of the billiard room one Saturday morning when Duck was cheekier than usual. The louts waiting for the SP bookmaker to arrive hung out there. Eventually Gutsa Mevinney pulled Duck's pants down and spat on his dick, then pretended to fuck Duck up the arse. Duck's language got fouler and Gutsa got rougher till he got a horn. The two-and-sixpenny punters egged him on, and because he was about as bright as a 20-watt globe Gutsa responded. He had the flange of his prick into Duck before the kid's real screams made the gamblers realize Gutsa was really poo-jabbing the boy. Then they pulled him off.

"That's what Tony Delarue calls corn-holing."
"Gutsa'd fuck anything with hair on it."
"He's already had a go at the barber's floor."
"Don't worry about anything Duck says," Jerry said. "Mum says he suffers from a lack of love. She says real love matters more than phony affection."
"Grandad says Duck's like his old man . . . all piss and wind and easier to knock over than a schooner. Would you really go to Sydney?"
"I want to go somewhere . . . away from here. You're the only one I'd miss."
"It's funny, Jerry. I never want to leave here. I'm gonna get a job as soon as I get my Intermediate Certificate at High School."
"Grandad might have something to say about that."
"He will! So will I," Monte said cocksuredly. "I wanta start earning money so I can look after him in a few years' time. I'll get round him somehow." He hunched his collar-bones. "Hey, Jerr . . . nick up the tap and refill this watering can." He was never sure when he was as positive as he often pretended to be.

"You know, Grandad," he once said, determined to get a sensible answer, "Peter Pan had the right idea. I mean . . . exactly what am I going to do when I'm too old to race round the Terribana Hills with the gang, campin' in the lantana . . . fightin' with Duck?"

"You'll still be too young to get drunk," Grandad said. "Maybe you'll decide to climb a mountain. You'll be amazed how soon one of those can crop up when you need one."

Monte opened his mouth.

Grandad reached forward and closed it gently, saying, "Words can't solve everything in this world, Boy."

He put an arm around the old man's shoulders. "I'm glad we're livin' in the same times, Grandad."

"That's a nice way to put it," Grandad said.

"It *was* a nice damn thing for me to say, wasn't it? So how about a full jigger of rum in my tea tonight?"

"Don't get too big for your sandshoes."

"Would you honestly give me a hidin' if I was stinkin' bad some time?"

"Boy, if you were wrong enough I'd strop you within an inch of your life."

"You would!" Monte's eyes were like antennae. Then he grinned generously. "Yous Singletons sure are something surprisin'."

"Ewes are female sheep," Grandad said.

At times Monte endeared himself deliberately to people with a toothy approach and a polite cobbled tone.

"You got more teeth than a bike's sprocket wheel," Duck said, and almost lost one of his own.

"Let me carry that bag for you, Mrs. Harmon," Monte said. "It looks too heavy for a little lady like you to lug . . ."

"Here's a couple more stamps, Mr. Carney. They're from Ceylon. I won 'em off Kenny Leslie at pothole . . ."

"Found your cat, Mrs. Stewart. Swanton's dog had it cornered in Garside's fernery. I booted it . . . oh, not your cat, the dog . . ."

"You look nice today, Miss Bowen. Kinda actressy like Barbara Stanwyck. Nobody would ever think you were an Infants School Headmistress."

"I'll accept that as a compliment, Boy, and not as innuendo."

"You can wind words better than most women can wind wool, Miss Bowen."

He could infuriate them just as easily.

"And where are you going to all dressed up, Master Howard?"

"Up to the Chadla Reservoir for a drink, Mrs. Harmon."

"I hear poor old Grandad wasn't feeling so well last week, Monte."

"I haven't heard that one yet. Mr. Carney. And we ain't poor and he isn't old!"

"That's a nice shirt, son. I'd like to get my boy one just like it. Do you know where Grandad got it?"

"Yep! At the gettin' place, Mrs. Stewart."

"Congratulations, Boy. They tell me you guessed the number of peas in the bottle at the bazaar."

"I'll tellya, Mrs. Garside . . . the truth. I saw Miss Bowen filling that oyster bottle with peas: she put tissue paper in the middle of it. So I pinched the leftover packet and counted the number of peas left in it. Then I bought a packet just like it. I had to be close."

"That was dishonest!"

"It was, wasn't it? She sure shouldn't have padded the middle of that bottle with tissue."

"I meant you were dishonest, Montgomery Howard."

"Well . . . games of chance are against the law anyhow . . . except for the Catholic raffles."

He could be helpful, too.

"Monte, honey? This is a list of local native birds' eggs I need for a big window display at Christmas. Can you help? I'm told the ibis's egg will be impossible to get these days." He stood at attention when Goldie Killorn stopped him and spoke to him. The sparkling Miss Killorn could enthrall men and could keep young boys enslaved.

Monte looked the list over soberly, hoping a lot of people would see him with this scintillating lady. "You can't blame the ibis for keeping away from the Wollbung swamp," he said. "Have you taken a look at it lately?"

"Not at all . . . recently," Goldie said, her ivory-plated smile whittled in amusement.

"Even the leeches will be pulling out of the swamp soon," Monte said. "But what if I lend you my Uncle

Mitch's egg collection? I've added to it a bit. Did you know my Uncle Mitch?"

"I did," Goldie said. "I had a crush on him when I was your age."

"You did?"

"And your Dad had a crush on my sister, Maudie."

Monte had heard the verb on Maudie Killorn.

"You know, Phyllis, there was something funny about the way Maudie Killorn died. She *did* have a goiter, but it wasn't that. I believe septicemia . . ."

"An abortion?"

"I didn't say that."

Goldie leant over and kissed the kid's forehead. "You're a doll." Monte hadn't heard that one before and it bewildered his throbbing heart.

He could hold his own against the worst when it came warted in Gutsa Mevinney. "If it ain't ol' Freckleface 'Oward with Pretty Little Kylie." Gutsa blocked their paths with clodhoppers as big as Feet-Feet's. "Where you two Dinkies goin'? Up the cook's cunt lookin' fer doughnuts?"

"If ya wanta know," Monte said, "we're on the way up the camel's arse lookin' for the desert but didn't know we'd come across shit so soon."

"Not so fast!" Gutsa made a scrum move that was quick for him, considering he was a lousy Rugby Union player.

"Git outa the way," Monte said, "or I'll hike back to the cop shop an' tell 'em you bum-fucked Duck Allsop."

"Fuck off and take the piss-pot with you," Gutsa said. Jerry was a word for chamberpot.

"Let's talk about the Great Australian Passion . . . for nicknames," Miss Cruikshank said. She chalked it on the blackboard like an excited traffic sign. Perhaps her only passion was for capital letters. "Now give me some ideas you can mull over the weekend."

"That we can mull over during the weekend!" Elizabeth Griffin said.

Ignoring Elizabeth, the teacher waved her hand at Swiftie. "Terry Madison. Instead of fiddling with that shanghai, give us a thought."

"It's a gongai," Swiftie said. "I mean that's the name for a shanghai which is another name for a catapult . . . that Mr. Delarue calls a slingshot." He was intrepid without being insolent.

"Don't try too hard to be clever," Cruikshank said, not angrily but holding her hand outstretched to indicate she was confiscating the gongai.

Desperate, Swiftie tried to sidetrack her. "It's pretty hard for me now, Miss Cruikshank. Ever since you gave me those lines on Jonathan Swift the kids all call me 'Swiftie.'"

After the kids had had their giggle, she said with her dowagerial smile, "And I'm told that you glory in it." How can other children realize that she doesn't mean to be unfair just because she loves one pupil intensely? "I'm sorry," she said, "but it won't be as easy for George Trabels to go through life being called Gulliver." She dropped her hand.

"It's better than Gullible," Georgie said.

"I have a cousin in Chadla called Deefa," Janet Tolby said. "She can't do a thing about it, but."

"Any more than I can do about your 'buts,' Janet." She was just as anxious as the kids for the bell to ring today, but she was suddenly curious. "Deefa?"

"Dee-for-Diane! That's her real name. Diane Marion . . ."

"Oh, my God . . . I mean, poor child." Kate Cruikshank inhaled. "So! Do we think we are clever? Do we get personal satisfaction? Do we feel secure with a nickname? Is it a sign of popularity or not? Are we sadistic about such things?"

"Sadie Who? Sadie Woo! Who's Sadie Woo?" Duck jabbered away for a laugh.

"Jerry Kyle," Miss Cruikshank said, "do you have anything to say cleverer than Francis Allsop's inane Chinese horse?" Getting her own laugh helped.

Jerry stood up — something only the girls usually did when answering. "I think if we don't have a nickname we feel cheated."

Monte shot up his hand. "I think the unfairest thing is when we make private jokes about people who don't know what their nickname is."

"Go . . . on . . . you are, at least, being original." Cruikshank was intrigued by a secret feeling that she knew what was coming. But would he dare?

"Miss Cruikshank."

"Yes?"

"Well, I think . . . Miss Cruikshank, it's only fair that you should know what they're calling you this year."

There was a forty-lung gasp.

"Go on." Kate could be seductive when necessary.

"Well . . . it's . . . Quasimodo."

A silence deeper than the Mindanao. Monte was determined to hold his guilty breath longer than anybody else. Whatever that proved.

Cruikshank smiled. "Thank you, Boy Howard. I'm glad that someone is reading their Hugo." The bell went and there was an explosion of breath, and distinct tears in each of Monte's eyes. "I'll let *you* in on a secret. My favorite nickname was given to me by your Uncle Mitchell, who loved his Shakespeare. It was Richard the Third. Class dismissed!"

Monte did not avert his eyes as he went past her: his teacher had the right to see those tears. She nodded subtly to him, saying, "It's all right; I never expected to be called Esmeralda."

7

IT WAS NOT BECAUSE Monte found life dull; but at least once a year the Satan in him would take over and he'd think of some diabolical scheme to keep the gang busy.

He did not see himself as supreme among them. Batter was not only the best cricketer in the school but a Valley Soccer Representative Under-13. For his age, Gloamy was a mechanical genius and could already take a motorbike engine and gear box apart and reassemble them. He could also magnify the attraction of a small Christmas tree with a colorful pulse of light, buying a few tinted torch globes and an elevenpenny battery from Woolworths. Then there was the magnetic Swiftie, the most popular kid in town. People liked him; women adored him. He was not pretty-pretty like Jerry Kyle, just sickeningly handsome.

"He reminds me of a young Tyrone Power."

"Goldie Killorn had his photo in the Children of the Valley display in Kincomba and people kept asking where he lived."

"Especially *girls*."

"Swiftie says his ambition is to fuck himself to death before he's thirty."

"That old?"

Terry Madison was one of those boys who come along every generation or so and flourish in the warmth of everyone's hopeless affection. Some of these young princes never realize just how completely loved they are, just how wholesale their charm. Pocket-Lotharios with ageless appeal, scissoring manners and the ability to make paper patterns of other people's defenses.

"When that kid smiles at me, Muriel, I feel funny in the fanny."

"His dear little shining eyes light up my day," Mr. Rowlandson said, playing pocket billiards.

"Come here, Swiftie," Feet-Feet said. "Nibble me clit and let me suck your love-joint and I'll give ya sixpence."

But his three mates figured that Monte had more of what they wanted most . . . unlimited freedom. This intrigued them. There was also a slight mysticism about him: the truth — he could live without them. They knew they were second to his pigeons; and, young as they were, sensed they might be drifters without him.

One night at a secret gang meeting Monte suggested that all lavatories in Boomeroo leaning beyond the seventy-ninth degree were to be bowled over—all except Granny Brough's quaint diddy which nested in chickweed and, draped by morning glories and weed-ivy, was shaded by the last remaining lillipilli tree in town.

"If Granny Brough's old shithouse comes down there'll be poop and morning glories all over our lillipilli tree," Swiftie said. "Besides, she's always good for homemade bickies when ya starvin'."

"It leans more than the bloody Tower of Pisa," Gloamy said.

"I'll go along with it," Batter said, "unless she starts spittin' on the lillipillies."

Every year when the berries were ripe the gang held its

rites beneath the tree at midnight, and they dreaded that Granny Brough might become a monster like Granny Green if she found out. Granny Green was no dear little old lady-passing-by. When the grapevine disguising her fernery came to life each year she went round spitting on the ripening grapes three or four times every day, to discourage the kids from stealing them at night.

"Not just little-old-lady spits either." Duck reported. "They're real dirty big old snotty gollions. All yellow muck. Ya can pick the bones out of 'em!"

"I'll give them young hooligans more'n a bellyache," she chortled.

"Give'm-shit-Granny-give'm-shit," her cockie cackled.

Granny Green was ninety-nine and in spite of her dreadful antique clothes she looked forty years younger than Granfarver Jones who was ninety. She evidently had a health secret but nobody knew what it was.

"They reckon she lets her dogs lick her thing . . . would that help?"

They called their scheme Operation Dunny in honor of Errol Flynn's glorious screen war career.

"All we need is Errol along."

"Aw . . . he'd just pick up some sheila and root her under the shithouse trellises while we did all the hard yakka."

"I wouldn't mind havin' the hard he's got in his pants," Swiftie said. "I bet he's got a dong a foot long . . . fat as a hippo's. I bet he can fuck like . . ."

"Down, boy, down," Gloamy said, patting Swiftie's crotch where his prick was responding to his own Flynn-talk.

"I don't care what they say about the way you can use it," Swiftie said. "A big prick has gotta be better!"

"Listen to Loverboy," Batter said. "Ties a hanky round his balls at night now to get them to hang lower."

"Oh, do you, doll?" Monte quipped, stroking Swiftie's

cheek and using Goldie Killorn's Americanism for the first time.

"You're asking for it," Swiftie said.

"That's what the salami said to the old lady when she got the butter out to make a wog sandwich," Gloamy said.

"Come on, let's get on with Operation Dunny and quit all this baloney," Monte said, laughing crazily at his own joke.

They made a three-ply angle-piece of one hundred and one degrees so that no disputed dunny was destroyed by mistake. If it leant more than this angle it was doomed. Thumbs down! NERO.

"One hundred and one *exactly*," Monte said.

In the next several weeks quite a few dunnies met their oozy fate. The Operation Dunny Vigilantes measured, heaved and yelled. Don Quixote should have had it as good with windmills. In the quiet comfort of their living rooms husbands and wives looked at each other in listening dismay when they heard, close by, hurled on the night air, the clear boyish cries of "NERO." And over went another lavatory while the Lillipilli Raiders capered off leaving a wake of glistening shit. Success was too much for them; it went to their heads like Enos bubbles until excess was not enough.

Some couples were even more perturbed the following morning when they made their liverish pilgrimage down the back yard and found their dunny absolutely pooped out.

"John! Get up! John? It's lying on its side . . . and *it's* everywhere."

"What, fer Chrissake?"

"The . . . lavvie. It's fallen over and . . . well . . . the mess is everywhere. The poop! John, it smells something awful."

"Well, whose shit don't stink?"

"Will you *get up* and do something about it?"

"What the Bejesus can I do with a back yard fulla shit if it's like you say?"

Trouble was, there were more dilapidated dunnies in Boomeroo than there were moonless nights in the valley that year; so it became a dangerous war game in the hot, anodized moonlight. The intruders' pearl-light shadows were almost as shackling as sun shadows. Their furtive movements were straight out of movie cartoons: it was unbelievable that four bodies could become so laminated behind a fence post or so glued to one slim tree trunk.

Though outlaws, their principles were firm, and when Lightfoot's lavvie was reviewed and sentenced to topple, Gloamy Lightfoot learnt that to be a Lillipilli Raider in this fray meant going all the way with no time to pray . . . not even with a constipated future looming. "I didn't think it meant we'd push our own shithouses over," he complained.

"Yours, not ours!" The other raiders raised their voices in cynical unison.

"If you need a poop tomorrow," Batter said just before the deed was accomplished, "you can use my dunny for a tray-bit."

"Up you," Gloamy said. "I'll kangaroo in the storm-water channel if I have to."

"Wanna be careful," Monte said. "Heralda Leslie's often down there with her sketch pad."

Batter nearly pissed himself elaborating on that, and between gusts let them in on it.

"If we go to Kincomba Show next year . . . hah . . . we'll see Gloamy's dick . . . arrrrrah . . . on onea the art prizes, lookin' like a snail ona willow tree . . . oh-shit . . . with . . . er . . . a First Prize ribbon pinned right through it . . . an' . . . ahahaha . . . it won't be for bein' the biggest!"

"Shut up, you grub, or I'll tie ya prick t'ya big toe."

"Hey! Don't go givin' Swiftie ideas how to stretch *his* prick."

"Well, come on," Gloamy said. "Let's git it over with.

We're lucky my old lady ain't inside, 'cause she nelly always goes for a poop before she goes to bed." He kicked Batter in the shins. "Come on you funny-fuckin' bastard . . . heave!" These two loved each other with a depth they would probably never experience again in their lifetimes.

They left Holman's till last because it sat on a rise at the end of town on the corner of Main Road and Harvard Street, leaning towards the main street, with an excellent view of the police station. It was obvious that when this particular catastrophe happened it was going to impede traffic the next morning. Also, it was common knowledge that little Arnie locked himself in for hours after dark playing with himself. It was a disaster worth looking forward to, and it happened *exactly* as predicted. Arnie emerged unscratched but covered in shit . . . with a new name he wore for the rest of his life, Poopy Holman — and his children were all, for ever, Little Shits.

Apart from Granny Brough's, the only dunny to escape their trial by geometry was Allsops' because there was hardly enough of it to warrant the Nero treatment. "Give Duck a few more weeks and there won't be enough left to push over."

At that time it had become Duck's source of the morning's wood, which he had to get each night so that his mother could start the fuel stove next day. Duck had begun by ripping off every fourth or fifth weatherboard, then every second or third, until the shithouse now looked more latticed than lived in.

Finally, when the exposure bothered her more than the draught, Mrs. Allsop, realizing who the culprit was, grabbed the nearest weapon — the last stanchion supporting the backhouse where it sloped toward Aldertons' chicken coop — and chased her son along Main Road yelling, "I'll belt the mutton out of you, my boy!"

When mother and son returned home exhausted, supporting each other, the structure had collapsed. It had relaxed on top of the next-door fowl house, discharging the few intercepting palings and triggering Duck's hinge. The dirty big black retriever was already in the Aldertons' hen pan, wrestling with Mrs. Alderton in the chicken shit, while the fowls she had come to rescue had escaped into Allsops' and were already foraging around in the crap from the deceased dunny.

It was on again. This time Duck headed for the creek while his mother, knowing the stanchion was altogether useless now, went after him with inspired strength and splintered the old plank across his retreating bum, screaming. "Come back here, you bugger-of-a-boy, and fix this lavatory or I'll get your father to rub your nose in it when he gets home."

Rallying, Mrs. Alderton, rather than be raped by the dirty big black retriever, joined in the Duck-hunt and left her chooks to a dog worse than kismet.

Pursued by these two harridans, Duck made the other side of the Dooragul, hardly wetting his ankles.

This finale made Operation Dunny a liberal legend — Duck's lambasting sometimes the beginning of it, sometimes the spiking end, and always the howl of it. After checking his dictionary, Monte declared it to be an active and moral contribution to the beautifying of Boomeroo. It made the town diddy-conscious and the MacDonald Township brickyards did a blazing business for months. Some people put in septic tanks, and some even applied to Council for permission to dig a *sceptic* system.

A year later, when many householders had spent money on their back yard chateaux and reorganized their sanitary habits, Kincomba extended the sewerage system up the valley. Later, Wollbung Charlie, the last of the Chinese market gardeners in the valley, who had previously cultivated only the perimeter, leased the defunct Sanitary Depot and grew even bigger and better, whiter and riper, tastier and more, Japanese onions . . . to sell in Kincomba.

"Herro, Charleee! You mi'yonaire velly soon, you yellow bastard! Have enough dough to send old body home to China in gland style, eh?"

"Me no Chinese! He Hong Kong Blitish. Me git bellied 'ere like fair-dinkum-fuckin' Aussie and leave money for my fliends to git fair-fuckin'-dinkum *drunk* . . . like good Ilishman."

"Wonder what Confuscius'll have to say about that, Charlie?"

"Con-fuckin'fucius say: Man who dig in Aussie shit end up very fuckin' rich poofter," Charlie said precisely.

"That woman on the Kincomba wireless Home-lovers' Hour said to turn your old-new outdoor toilet into a tool shed."

"Silly old bitch," Duck said. "All the kids know that. Where else'd ya go to play wiff ya tool!"

In those green dream days children knew as much as they learnt from one another but very little about the paraphernalia they might find hidden in their parents' bedrooms.

"Li'l Peterdunny's eight and still thinks it's to piddle out of," Swiftie said one day when they were discussing the age a boy ought to be before or when he realized the acts of life if not some of the more detailed facts.

"It's not the fucking I don't understand," Gloamy said. "It's the moony way they get when they say they're in loooooove. Lookin' into each other's eyes and playin' handsies, and all that crap."

"An' nibblin' on each other's necks," Batter said. "Gee! You ever notice the bloody big love bites on some of those sheilas that work in the Store?"

"I'm just gonna fuck and fuck and fuck," Swiftie said.

"None of that love stuff for me. I'll go up with the blind one morning like that guy in the yarn."

"Hey! Can't those little cock sparrows fuck, but?"

"What about wild ducks?" Monte said. "I saw about fifteen drakes get onto one poor old duck over the swamp at the end of the matin' season. She musta been the only female not nestin' . . . and they fucked and fucked 'er till she couldn't even wobble away any more. Onto 'er and onto 'er again and again. Most of them three times or more each. They fuckin' near killed 'er. I don't think any woman could take that much from a football team. I pulled meself off just watchin' 'em at it." The great confession.

At sprinkled times they had all watched lovers screw in certain popular lantana bowers in the Terribana Hills, although they weren't dedicated rock-spiders like Duck.

"I saw Young 'Enry Garside whoppin' it up one of Medowie's cows before he got married," Duck said. "And the cow kept mooin' like as if it was being milked by Goldie Killorn."

"I reckon we're lucky our balls don't get caught up like a dog's, but."

"Fancy havin' Duck's dirty big black retriever's balls caught up inside you."

"Don't that make you glad you're not a bitch in this town?"

They agreed to that. Their frenzy was so coarse you wouldn't want to wipe your arse on it.

"But why do all the grubs and molls act shoofty-like when they wander up to the hills on Sundays?"

" 'Cause they're mostly with someone else's missus."

"Billie Hawke's missus's always with someone else, and someone different."

"Bejesus, have you seen her at it? Don't she jump around some and get excited when they're fuckin' er. I thought at first, when I saw her with Upsa Downey, he must've laid 'er on a bully-ants' nest."

"What's these lover's balls Gutsa's always goin' on about?" Gloamy shuffled about rubbing his balls and moaning the way Mevinney did. " 'Jezeers! Couldn't git inta this moll last night. Lyin' bitch said she 'ad the rags on, an' I've 'ad lover's balls all day.' " He sidled over to Swiftie and grabbed one of his hands to press to his crotch. "Any you kids wanna jack me off?"

"Aw, quit your molling around," Swiftie said. He was getting short-tempered about such boyish irrelevantics these days. "I'm sick of sneakin' a feelin' here and there of those little flat titties at school. Wish I could get into a proper juicy pussy meself."

They learnt what they could from farm and back yard beasts and from two-legged animals like Gutsa and sluts like Big Fat Nellie; from moral and immoral men and women who inhabited their lives. Older brothers and sisters came nearest to reliable sources.

"Hey, Doffie, I thought you told me you couldn't get a girl preggie the first time you ever fucked 'er."

"I said the chances were a million to one."

"Well, ain't I the lucky bastard? Wish I'd taken a lottery ticket instead."

It was the evolution of sexual conjecture in a vague and sometimes evil form. Not often, but here and there, someone with compassionate memories would help a child grow up untouched by this spread ignorance.

Swiftie almost always concluded the gang's discussions with, "Anyhow, the lottaya're jealous because I got the biggest dick." Bet on it!

"Cricket's better," Batter said.

"An' takin' an engine apart," Gloamy said.

"Trappin' finches and flyin' pigeons," Monte said.

Swiftie was never convinced. Literature on the subject

was sparse this side of Vonnie Kyle's bookcase — with all the hot stuff hidden under Feet-Feet's sturdy bed — and Goldie Killorn's renowned copy of *Fanny Hill*, which half the town knew about and elaborated upon.

"That Fanny Hill would've been run out of Kings Row," Mrs. Allsop said. Kings Row was her moral yardstick and the older she got the shorter it became.

"I once asked me Dad if we had the edge on women."

"Yeah . . . and what did 'e say?"

"No; but that at times women had a funny sorta way of blamin' themselves for what went wrong with a marriage . . . especially when they wanted *it* badly. He said to wait till they were beggin' for *it* and willin' to blame themselves for everything . . . and *then* agree with them that everything *was* their fault . . . then to give it to 'em like as if you was Errol Flynn takin' another cherry."

"How should it be with a woman?" Young Moroney asked his father a week before he got married.

"Don't expose your impatience," the counseling daddy said, harrumphing.

"Christ, if Young Moroney exposed his impatience he'd be arrested. His weapon's thicker than Mrs. Allsop's skin and half as long as Young Henry's . . ."

. . . which still makes it imposing.

> *Long and thin goes too far in*
> *and irritates the ladies:*
> *Short and thick does the trick*
> *and manufactures babies.*

"I guess you need a woman to make a baby," Monte said one evening as darkness crept into the house and surrounded the kitchen's fireglow.

"You do," Grandad said. "And she needs you."

"Yes, but who's the most important?"

"Why, the baby of course."

Early some mornings, when his mind was awake but his eyes still asleep as if blacking out the coming dawn, Monte masturbated in a swelter of bodies. Sometimes he implanted himself upon Vonnie Kyle's breasts while others fought for the most genuine sexual facet of her body. Once Gutsa lay beside him fucking Duck, and Duck was enjoying it. Another time Feet-Feet entertained — and handled — three young bloods with Goliath pricks right there in his bed. The Gorgon Eternity Smith often consoled him, but she was no tooth fairy and left no money. Usually Swiftie ended up at the foot of the bed admiring his manner and adoring his balls.

"Shit, I wish I could screw like you, Monte. Wish I had your heavy danglin' loaded balls. A prick's no good unless you've got the danglers to produce the spoof to fill 'em up."

"Kiss me arse an' I'll tellya me secret, Maddo." It was measureless to be as expert as Monte Flynn. "Errol told me all his secrets . . . that's my secret. So go wear ya hand out, Swiftie!"

8

THE STREETS WERE the barometer of the social climate of Boomeroo. This didn't mean that if you went to a Leslie party or a Garrison fun-party, or an intellectual bash at the Griffith's, you would find a rash of pale women clipped from the society columns of the *Woman's Weekly* or the Sydney Sunday papers. But the town did have its different strata of living.

" 'Social,' Miss Cruikshank?"

" 'Social' is both an adjective and a noun. A simple enough word. As a noun it generally means a gathering of people for some happy occasion. In this town one would expect to have less fun at a social than at a party. As an adjective, it will be enough for now if you think of it as a certain way of life in a community. Later on you can expand on this as you yourselves grow and take part in these gatherings."

High Street was above Main Road and Reserve Terrace was below it on the banks of the creek. Pacific Avenue was on the higher perimeter of the town and its keen-arrised, gable-eyed homes spied down upon the roofs of lower Boomeroo. Creek Road on the far side of the Dooragul ran parallel to the railway line: people preferred to pretend that it was a part of Wollondonga, that inglorious place of cubby-like houses clustering the pit.

"Wollondonga's all over the place like a mad woman's piss."

On its way east to Chadla, Main Road became Rugby Drive and ran past the Union football fields between both towns, after winding through a mile of wild bush known as Kraigee Run. In the opposite direction Main Road merged into the Highway where it headed towards the mountains. Half a mile out of town on this climb it was intercepted by Eton Drive, the road to Bora Bora, still referred to as Gutshaker Road, its old bullocky name.

There was no social stock in Boomeroo: not even the powerful Leslies were considered class.

"No stock! No stock *at all* in any of those Northside-nothing towns," vowed Mrs. Adam Garrold-Herald of Kincomba, the indebted valley's doyen Debrett, when a wayward daughter married (and later divorced) Ben Leslie.

"My dears," Sharon Garrold-Herald Leslie said at her homecoming reception — divorce papers in one hand, Shooting Sherry in the other, and a quarter-of-a-million settlement between her teeth — "at a do I gave for Ben's friends' wives they *ate* the cinnamon sticks I gave them to stir their coffee with."

"Listen, Beryl," Mrs. Allsop said. "You know that Mrs. Adam Garrold-Herald with the needle tongue? Her husband's a runner. I know things about *him* you wouldn't even hear on the wireless in Big Sister, and *she'd* be run out of Boomeroo if she lived here." Henrietta Arden Allsop herself was the grub's Debrett.

"Mrs. All-arse should live in Kings Row with Ann Sheridan and Ronald Reagan; and Claude Rains ought be given an extra sharp knife."

8 I

"I like to listen to 'Those Feveral Girls' on the wireless, myself, Ena. Of course, they'd sleep anywhere but a manger."

"Those Feveral Girls" was a long-running suds-serial about five sisters who had lost count of their own husbands but married one another's with an abandon that seemed to delight their nong-nong parents, to dismay and delight their listeners, and surely must have deceived their sponsors.

Money provided a pseudo-social level but engendered no real ill will. Money was so bloody indiscriminate.

"Cash is the best religion because you don't have to go to church to make it . . . but a little prayin' helps at times!"

"An Abo's quid's as good as a miner's any day."

If you had enough to stop caring you lived on Pacific Avenue. Not exactly rich and still worried a bit? You lived on High Street. You most likely lived on one of the cross streets if you were satisfied but not quite happy with what you had, or if you were happy but a little dissatisfied with what was coming your way. These streets were named University, Church, Cambridge, Scots, Harrow, Radley, Kings, Harvard. The new few modern postwar groups, building their own homes, lived in caravans and meantime garages on the ninth unnamed cross street, already being spoken of as Yale . . .

"Bloody Tony Delarue started that!"

"Ruby," the ever-aiming Allsop said, "we got the best-educated-sounding streets in New South Wales, but what goes on along them after dark they don't teach in school. The kids go for a drive in a borrowed car, park on another street between the corner lamps, and then there's ructions because some little tabby gets up the stick."

"She shoulda got the stick at school instead."

Like most gossipers, Mrs. Allsop is not entirely wicked. She is even loved:

"I'd ravver me Mum belt me because she can't hit as 'ard as me Dad."

She is also hated:

"That woman talks so much shit: if she had a tongue in her arse she'd nag herself to death."

She is human:

"Don't give sorrow to children if you can help it, Ernestine. They get enough cruelty from other kids to prepare them for the sadness they're sure to encounter later in life."

She is not common like her closest, oldest frienemy, Liz'n Linda:

"Don't talk to me about your mates . . . I know what mates do. They fuck each other! Mostly up."

She is immutable:

"Let me put it to you in black and white: that woman is as scarlet as they come."

She is loyal:

"Liz'n Linda [and the whole town knows that Linda has been listening to the all-knowing for over twenty years], I know my Reggie can be a big prick at times but nobody else in this town had better try and ram it down my throat."

She has entered upon this scene, she has acted, she has spoken, and some day she will leave, and her God alone is entitled to judge her.

If Boomeroo's native happiness is based on beer or bastardry, apples or arguments, coal or cattle-dogs, what does it matter? If you thought that God filling your soul was as important as His filling your belly, surely you wouldn't be convinced of His Universal Lambency by someone who was hungry as hell?

"Someone's going' to towel you up if you keep asking mud-arse questions like that."

"An' if ya sound too much like Eternity Smith you're gonna git a cock in ya tonsils."

* * *

Monte's rambling two-storied kingdom was at the bottom of the big back yard, beyond the lavatory, which itself was a trek. Before you got to the ducket you crossed a resected six-foot rib of yard as suggestive of a moat as anything could be. Whatever blew, flew, grew, fell or was thrown in that bare borderland was destined to be burnt in a forty-four-gallon drum incinerator behind the dunny. A no-man's-land.

At the top of his building a rickety door opened. Set off by straining wires and weights, this closed an inner door. The second door, sprung loose, closed and locked the first. At the Kyle-fence end of the ducket Jerry's recently designed trapdoor allowed Monte a shoofty freedom — even from Grandad — which he had never had before. It was begun as a gimmick thing, more complicated than Monte's original door, and it pleased them to share its secret.

Monte opened the observatory-type roof in the center section and flushed the nineteen birds he had in training. They would use the singular lightweight traps on returning. The tumbler tossed its head and shunted away from him, blinking its heliograph eyes. It was a bloody guts and gobbled its food and Monte often vowed to send it to Mt. Isa, that Siberia of Boomeroo legend. One night he dreamt he did this and saw it falling out of the basket on the railway station, giving the liberator a fat-feathered shock, nesting in the waiting room and shitting on the ladies' hats. As they whacked at it with their brollies he woke up laughing. "You silly fat bird . . . lucky Sarey Gamp wasn't there."

Monte had a personal regard for most of the Dickens characters he had read about — particularly Mr. Jingles, Sam Weller, Mrs. Pickwick, The Artful Dodger, Steerforth, and Sydney Carton.

"That Sydney Carton seems like he belongs to now, Grandad."

"He sure would be at home in the Sulphide pub."

"Not just his drinking . . . I mean, he seems modern."

"I think what Dickens knew for sure, Boy, was that times change more than people."

When the fluttering petered out and the last shed feather airy-fairyed round him, Monte watched his birds circle, a single blue and white visage creating an ever-widening orbit — the sky like a Michelangelo ceiling. Satisfied that none had settled on any of the nearby roofs, he checked his mothering birds, which he would exercise later. Five hens with younguns had separate pens.

The mealy hen was nursing two by the mosaic-pied cock. A red-check had hatched out one egg by the mosaic-pied cock and one (he believed) by his blue-bar cock champion . . . Grandad would never have allowed that to occur in his flying days. This was the hen that would not settle down during the day.

The kid did things his own way, and though Grandad sometimes shook his thoughts with comments on his methods he never actually interfered. "I got to hand it to you, Boy, you have some original ideas, and who's to say they won't work out?"

There was a blue-check hen with two squeakers by his new blue-check cock, the bird he bought with five pounds prize money from a Murwillumbah win. One of these looked as sickly as a squab could look and still survive.

The mother of his blue-bar cock champion was a magnificent specimen of Grandad's breeding program. A blue-bar herself, her pedigree went as far back as the chest-high heap of exercise books in Grandad's bedroom. Now she was nursing two younguns from another blue-check cock that had been showing great form. She was a perfect parent and nourished her squeakers with blooded devotion.

Finally there was a little blue-check hen raising a youngun from his blue-bar cock champion. She had come home one day with a tiny bloody stump where her left leg had been; so Monte rewarded her heroism by mating her belatedly with his best bird. So far she had only hatched one of her eggs.

"No hawk did that," Grandad said. "Someone with a gun did. You're lucky he was a rotten shot."

Monte had called her Boadicea after one of his few respected heroines. Only a couple of the hens had names. The mealy hen and the red-checker were his only birds with those distinctive colorings. The blue-check hen he had mated with the new blue-check cock was called Mrs. Gale after the fat neighbor next door, because she got pretty fat in the breeding season. The pigeon could lose weight in training; the neighbor never did.

"Mrs. Gale's fatter than Big Fat Nellie," Duck said. "Wonder what she'd giveya for a hot pie?"

"Somethin' like this," Monte said, discoloring one of Duck's enormous green eyes with a left he hadn't surmised could be so straight and strong.

"Aw, I don't fight southpaws," Duck said. "You're a lot of shoofty bastards. But tell me 'Owzza, howya pullya dick, right or left hand?"

"The way I do everything else . . . Ducksa . . . better'n you do!"

His champion blue-bar hen was called After-dark because on her first fly she hadn't clocked home until after the moon rose, smiling through foreboding clouds. Since then After-dark's records had been valuable.

Monte changed the red-checker over to an empty apartment downstairs where she might not be distracted from her younguns.

In another ground-floor compartment near the feed room he had an old retired pigeon called BHP. She had been his very first own pigeon and had won the Newcastle Fly, so he had called her after the mighty Newcastle steelworks. He felt sorry for BHP because he had an idea that homing pigeons had a Valhalla where they went if they died racing, which most of the best often did. "Like the early airmen, Grandad." This belief in Valhalla had helped him decide to fly pigeons for himself when Grandad gave it up.

"I really believe that pigeons have a sort of . . . Valhalla if they die flying, Grandad!"

"Then if you do, Boy, believe it! Don't ask me or the Headmistress or anyone else to substantiate it for you. There's no need to ever argue about religion if *you* have faith in one. What use would God be if you could take Him from a shelf when you felt like it and then mock Him after you had your mileage?"

For once Monte was silent in his guilt, because he was a great God-user . . . and he was also hung up on the idea (and sound) of Valhalla.

"Every Goddamn thing dies," Swiftie said. "Why not pigeons? I've seen a few cold stiff pigeons in parks in my time, and I figure they've been as dead as any pot-shot starling or stoned crow I've ever seen in the gutter."

"But I'm responsible for my birds."

"Then you ain't gonna work it out on paper like your homework," Swiftie said.

Monte had been to Sydney once and ever since firmly believed his birds *were* better off than the untrained bread-fed pigeons in that city's parks and squares. He had noticed some on an office roof close to the hotel, waddling on and off their precarious roosts, their whole world minute in the small window of his eye, their existence open to the huge grasp of the cold wind blowing through the chasm between the buildings.

"My birds are more like The Few who saved Britain."

"And the hawks are the Luftwaffe," Gloamy said. "Dududududuaaah!"

"Cut it out, you galah."

Monte went back up top and took the remaining unhatched egg from Boadicea: she fenced against his taking it; that was her duty. He had known for a few days it would never hatch, but swapped it gently from hand to hand in front of her as if to make her realize he was weighing his decision carefully. He took it out to the incinerator and broke it. It was rotten. Again he went back to the ducket, licked his indelible pencil as Grandad always had (it was his oldest recollectable memory) and made a note of the destruction in his pigeon register. Then he went and sat with Boadicea without saying a word to her for the rest of the training time before he whistled his birds in.

The pigeon whistle is odd, eerie and yet precise: kind of poetic in its eloquent immediacy; unbearable at a haphazard level. A projected note followed quickly by seven or eight jaunty quivers and quavers. Drone and trill and breathe deep. Monte's birds knew his whistle from Mr. Wright's on High Street and from Mr. Hadford's on Scots Street, and from Eee-ba-goum Ackeson's farther up Harrow. Monte had a windy strength. Mr. Wright was coughing something awful after five minutes. Sometimes Mr. Hadford had a blow-out and lost his false teeth at the same time as his patience and glasses.

Eee-ba-goum was a singing whistler and Monte envied him this talent. His own whistle had been copied from Grandad's and only the pigeons and Jerry Kyle knew the difference. But the birds came in that fraction sooner for Grandad because they had learnt he no longer had the unending perseverance he had taught his grandson. Grandad knew it was a true sport, a test of time and knowledge and complete dispassionate understanding. A relationship similar to that which a drover had to keep with his dog, with love a sentient dimension.

The pigeon whistle could set some people dreaming and drive others up the wall.

"Do they have to make that flamin' row?" Vonnie Kyle often complained.

"It's the proper whistle, Mum," Jerry explained. "It's a . . . an ability, Mum. Wish I could do it."

"I'll break your bloody neck if ya try!" Vonnie said, succinct as ever but not quite as loud as usual.

It soothed Mrs. Gale. Her late husband, Ernie, had flown pigeons in their courting days and many a Saturday afternoon she had spent in his ducket flat on her fat young back, a bag of pigeon peas under her bum, waiting for him to come into her tight, fat-muscled loins. Sometimes he pumped her for two hours before the spoof flowed.

"I always wanted a fat girl to fuck, to suck in my lovehoney, honey. I'm gonna fuck you for ever. Keep it up! Keep it up! Keep muscle-fuckin' me, honey. Then I'm gonna lay inside you, just love-dreamin' till the pigeons git here."

He was a great cunt man and also an immense talker.

Mrs. Gale gave the rocking chair another burst and inhaled the sensuous smell of the silverside she had steaming in the kitchen. She must give Grandad a hunk of it: the boy loved corned meat on his sandwiches.

Monte's whistle would arouse young Mrs. Garside from her honeymoon hangover and she became a ball of misguided energy as she tried to get the house into some sort of order before Young Henry arrived home from work to . . .

"Fork 'er!" Gutsa Mevinney said. "That's why Young Henry races home with his tongue between his legs every arvo. She's got hotter pants than the fellas workin' on the open hearth at the BHP steelworks."

Young Henry would inevitably find her disconsolately stabbing an uncooked roast or opening a tin of braised steak and onions, or simply crying in frustration.

"Poor biddy-darling," Young Henry said, hot to the seams of his overalls. "Let's go to bed for bumpy-boos, then we can go round to my Mum's for a bite to eat."

"Poor Henry," his doting Mum said. "Married to a lazy little bitch who can't butter bread. Sits on her backside all day eatin' lamingtons . . . that I make for *his* lunch, and readin' the *Woman's Weekly*. She's no good for anything."

Young Henry knew otherwise. His biddy-darling wife could adequately handle the biggest prick in the Lillipilli Valley . . .

"Horses included?"

. . . which in folklore almost choked Eternity Smith to death . . .

"And she never missed a breath when she gamarouched Donkey-boy Bousefield . . ."

. . . and excited the best whore in Chadla into giving him his money back.

Biddy-darling would be all for bumpy-boos and Young Henry would be dogging her and frogging her and bogging her with a piece of meat any butcher would be proud to hang in his window, quicker than she could have boiled a soft egg.

"Where the hell can she put it all?"

"It's a bloody sight nearly as big as my stallion's pissy-horn."

"Even Eternity said she'd never seen a revelation like it."

"I tell you, Olva, their honeymoon's goin' to run longer than *Gone with the Wind*."

"I've seen it eight times . . . just to see Ashley again."

"Ashley Wilkes was a ninny and would have been operated on in Kings Row."

Don't change the subject, and get to the sexual dearth of it.

"OK. Young Henry Garside's dong is so long it can eat grass."

"Why're you jealous, Pinhead? You got one big enough for half a man which is what you are!"

Young Henry's wife looked like a demure small girl,

and when they went walking she snuggled into him as if she was living on the smell of his armpits. At home she was someone else. Some afternoons Young Henry arrived home to find the half-cooked dinner in the garbage and a note on the kitchen table saying: *Meat* me in bed! He would stumble out of his overalls in the hallway, his shirt and singlet in the bedroom doorway, and by the time he got to the bedside his electrified love-joint was halfway to the pillows. In no time they were involved in the exuberant throes of one of their bumpy-boo games ranging from Mighty Joe Young and Terry Moore through Lex Barker and Jane, Robert Wagner and Natalie Wood, to Flash Gordon and Dale and Boris Karloff and Elsa Lanchester.

They were what some African tribes called the perfect combination: elephant man and gazelle woman. When little biddy-darling lifted her knees and spread her loins to meet the great fate her whole body melted beneath his, and where that ten and a half inches went was known only to her.

Even Young Henry never ceased to be amazed. Her moods ranged from lark-alive little animal to unnatural placid groveler and every one of her personalities pleased Young Henry. They hardly ever spoke except when he murmured, "Cunt-come?" This was his way of asking permission to bury his head in her crotch and slurp up her orgasm. The currency of their marriage was fucking, and she gave herself without discount. When her body was compressed between Young Henry and the mattress it was invisible, and when he was completely invaginated within her there was not one muscle or limb that her ultimately subdued body could move as she received his massive ejaculation. Even her fixed, glazed eyes were immovable as they looked beyond his shoulders to some inexhaustible paradise.

First thing every morning she gave him his piss-kiss to wake him; and after he came from the bathroom naked, before breakfast, she tongued what she called the sacred spot — his tiny untouched pink arse — and . . .

"Oh Henry, when I put my tongue into your bumhole it's as if I plug myself into a sex-electric power point."

. . . finally, before he left for work she sat on the hall table and, when he kneeled before her, held his thick coarse lips to her soft twat. No wonder Young Henry went off at 7 A.M. wishing it were already 4 P.M.

However, they were not absolutely the happiest couple in Boomeroo and their marriage certificate was not the iron-glad contract it should have been. Young Henry's Mum was one reason and Sadie's (heaven forbid, but that was her name) curiosity about smaller, jollier, more active pricks compared to Young Henry's starched monstrosity was the other. When Ben Leslie's curiosity about Sadie's capacity to accept all of Young Henry got the better of him and he arranged overtime for Young Henry, she was prime for the jolly action-fucking Ben was capable of.

Keeping a secret in Boomeroo was harder than hiding a Royal skeleton.

"Sadie'll soon know all about Ben's bag of tricks." And Ben Leslie's bag of tricks was not a metaphor. He carried enough paraphernalia in his Italian leather weekender to satisfy Caligula.

When his pigeons trapped in Monte fed them pigeon peas without waste but without being too economical. Pigeon peas are like hard brown pills specially grown to condition small bodies that are all feather, bone, muscle, head and heart. Those hearts could bring those small bodies up to eight hundred miles at cruising speeds of forty miles an hour. Taking advantage of tail winds, they could reach sixty-five. Battling a head wind they might have to rack along at twenty or even ten, but they were always heading home.

Between mountain peaks where hawks waited, above

towns where kids with airguns gleefully took pot-shots at them, over bush where some stupid hunter might batter them with a .22, they were always on the most direct way home. Their instinct could be dimmed by elemental factors, their wings, tired with distance, their spirits dampened by animal onslaught, but their hearts never flagged. This was courage. In Monte's case there may have been a tissue of love involved.

"That's about the only thing I think Grandad might be wrong about, Jerry. I love 'em and I think they know it." But he never coddled them or made pets of them. After a conditioning month in his ducket, no bird ever became a straggler.

"I'll grant you that," Grandad said. "You're the only flyer I ever heard of never had at least one or two stragglers a season."

Stragglers were wanderers: sometimes they came home a day or two late — or a week late; sometimes they came back months after a fly, as fat as a pet duck and with the nerve of a back yard rooster. With the exception of BHP and Mrs. Gale, Monte's birds each weighed about a pound and a half. They lived up to their name for the unerring ability to find their way home to their own small universe. When they arrived exhausted, Monte did sometimes lament over them without cuddling them.

"Why'dya have to fight the head winds?"

"Why di'n'tya go round the bushfires?"

"Oh God, why did it have to hail today?"

Yet Grandad had never heard the child cry since the night they had taken him away from his dying mother.

"Let him cry for the time being," the young nurse said. The midwife, old Nurse Lloyd, was out in the night ferreting a doctor.

"Bullshit, you stupid bitch," Vonnie Kyle said. "He isn't a calf lost in a paddock. Give him to me. Thank Christ you're not his mother! Your kids will grow up never knowing what a tit is. This baby's hungry . . . look!" She already had her ample breast to the baby's mouth. Vonnie was still breastfeeding Jerry at the time: she went ahead and gave the half-starved baby a . . .

"Gutbuster of a milkshake, that's what she gave him," Granfarver Jones always said.

Later that week, after Katharine, the young mother, had died, primarily from the sudden eight-month birth, Mrs. Kyle had his belly full and his face aglow with windy smiles; and Mrs. Gale fixed his bottles for Grandad and helped feed and raise him until he was out of nappies and into trouble.

"Was I a good baby, Grandad?"

"A good baby but a bugger of a kid!"

"I feel safe, livin' here with you, old man," Monte said, then deliberated. "How you reckon I stack up against my Dad or Uncle Mitch?"

"Well . . . you fly pigeons OK but you sure as hell can't paint furniture like Mitch could. And you're mutton compared to your Dad as a footballer."

"Aw, Grandad! Anyway, I don't paint furniture, I . . . decorate it."

"Son, you might decorate the floor while you're painting but you massacre furniture."

"I express myself . . . like Miss Cruikshank said we ought to."

"If you're quoting the *Bible* don't expect an argument from me," Grandad said.

"I might turn out to be a great artist one day . . ."

"Who massacres furniture!"

"Don't *you* get to be a fuddy-duddy."

"Watch it, Boy! I don't mind an occasional 'old man' but go easy on those 'fuddy-duddies.' "

"Now you're tying my shoelace . . . Any more puddin'?"

"Help yourself," Grandad said, passing the pudding bowl. "You know, you're likely to be a lot fuddy-duddier than me when you grow up. It happens."

"If that happens you can whale the livin' daylights out of me," Monte said.

In the gloaming of a smile, Grandad said, "I like that idea." The old fellow's gurgling was a ply of soft laughter and dreamy thought. It was also a ploy to distract from further comparisons to Chid Howard, the boy's Dad.

9

MONTE AND JERRY PASSED their High School examinations that year. This meant they had to catch the seven-thirty train to Kincomba each morning to go to Lillipilli Boys' High. Their crosses were that they had to wear the unbarrackable Cucumber school uniform — bottle green pants, white shirt, and green and white tie.

"You oughta moan!" Swiftie said. He had passed for Chadla Secondary Technical High. "I gotta wear a shitty-brown blazer and a yukkie yellow tie. An' all the drongos in town are goin' ta follow me round singin', 'Shit and yella for a rotten fella!'"

The majority of the kids from Sixth Class at Boomeroo Primary that year were going on to the new enormous complex, Kincomba Intermediate High School, and were happy and clubby about wearing a standard college gray uniform.

Girls like Elizabeth Griffith and Fenella Leslie who passed for the snobby Kincomba Girls' High were proud to wear striped red-and-blue accessories to their pleated navy blue Melbourne-made woolen tunics.

The last word Miss Cruikshank was asked to define was: "'Affluent'?"

"Wealthy. Abundant. An affluent society is a prosperous one concerned with material improvements." Her heart wasn't in it: this had been a good year for searchers. "Many affluent people are Philistines. Remember that, too, Fenella." They had had Philistine peppered into them early in the year. "You and Elizabeth might also remember that the noun 'affluent' also means a tributary. In a strict sense you will be running into bigger streams. God bless you. Don't forget everything you have learnt here. I know you will forget most of it. Try to retain a little. You have been a . . ." — She smiled; she had told them about Owen Wister's *The Virginian* once when someone had asked about the word "bastard" — ". . . bold class. But there is courage in boldness. Keep that courage. Good-bye."

"Good-bye, Miss Cruikshank."

No, not good-bye! Take my heart with you. Fill it with your youth and cunning and determination . . . and violence . . . and return it to me some day, refurbished . . . and beautified. Cruikshank was *not* a fuddy-duddy.

> *Oh to be once more among*
> *The beautiful and young*
> *. . . well-hung.*

My God, English is a ludicrous language. Here was a saintsend of young girls and a bucket of boisterous boys as full of life as a spend of sparrowlings in summer, and all they could say at the accumulation of six years' education was: "Good-bye."

Although he was now up at six thirty and home much later than from Primary School, Monte felt his promising young birds deserved all the time he could give them. He persevered and never minded what time he got away from the ducket in the evening.

Except for three short flys from Maitland, Newcastle

and Cockle Creek early in the season, his races were from the north. So naturally he loved the north wind, hated the southerlies and, like everyone else, detested the westerlies.

"Me Mum says pigs can see the wind," Duck said. He was a billy-boy in the sulphur shed at the cement works and had shot up suddenly, his thick neck busting out of his collars and his thickening dick bruising itself against the zipper of his new work pants. "Look . . . no more buttons on my fly!"

"So, what's the wind look like, Slops?" Gloamy said, calling Duck by his recently acquired billy-boy nickname which rhymed better with Allsop. The boy Duck Allsop grew (and grew) into the beer-sodden man, Slops Allsop.

The Southerly Buster was a bastard of a wind but the westerly was worse: it was a furnace from outback that sometimes blew pigeons out to sea, singeing them with its hot breath, and parching their endeavors. Summer evening southerlies were mild enough and cool enough, but the sudden, blowy Buster was wild and willful: its only purpose seemed to be to shock and destroy, and it gave no warning.

"Granfarver Jones once saw a Southerly Buster turn a chook inside out."

"That where he got all his shit from."

If a Southerly Buster ever hit on a flying Saturday Monte would curse it with billiard-room exuberance. His intra-State flys were from Walla Walla, Gwabegar, Narrabri, Murwillumbah, Armidale, Tenterfield, Lismore or Coolangatta. The Murwillumbah Fly was the earliest important indicator of most young pigeons' potentiality.

"These bloomin' birds see more of the country than we do, Grandad."

"That's because people gave up horses," Grandad said, "Once you would just saddle up, or hitch the sulky, and go. Or even take advantage of shanks's pony. But now people seem to have to pack for weeks before they even take the car out of the garage for a holiday."

> *Our Andy's gone with cattle now —*
> *Our hearts are out of order —*
> *With drought he's gone to battle now*
> *Across the Queensland border.*

"I love you, old man."

The Lillipilli Flying Season started in May with the Cockle Creek Fly and wound up in October with the long Mackay Fly. Mackay was far north on the Queensland Barrier Reef coast. Before the season opened officially the Lillipilli Federation members in Boomeroo, Bora Bora and Chadla flew their young birds on jaunts from Kincomba, Londonderry, Boolawoy, and sometimes from Shannondor and Killingworth, two soft-pulsed wine-growing centers across the Terribana Hills in the lovely snug vale of Goondigi.

Southern hemisphere birds matured quickly and a squeaker born in the spring could be trying his wings when only a little more than six months old. Some, the best, would fly through the longest, most grueling tests as yearlings.

A pigeon surviving the first hazardous season would probably fly for another two or three years. Hawks and bad weather and bushfires caused a lot of trouble, but the sudden storm punching around the South Pacific was their deadliest enemy. They pitted their pound and a half of guts against one of nature's most heartless moods and fought its force — which was capable of sending shipping to shelter, provoking a lake to madness or whipping a beach sandless — until they were nothing but battered featherless pulp. In flying history Down Under one great violent storm had been known to net a thousand birds in its elemental hysteria and scatter their bodies beyond the Coral Sea.

When Eee-ba-goum Ackeson first arrived from England he flew his birds as he had in the Old Country: up to two hundred miles the first year, maybe four hundred the next, and so on, until he realized these early maturing southland birds were strongest and healthiest and gutsiest (though less cunning) as yearlings.

"Like the young sheilas in the Islands. Some of them are women and can have kids by the time they're twelve."

As they got older even the champion birds grew crafty regarding hawks and other dangers and, in spite of their zeal, sometimes sought temporary refuge. But the good and girded young ones, with their eccentric intensity, matched their wings with anything above earth or below heaven.

A pigeon's egg hatched in about nineteen days. Monte's few squeakers had been born in a warm spring and these he encouraged during his first year at High School. He'd had more than his share of disappointment before Christmas. Mrs. Gale's two squeakers had to be destroyed because they had a deep canker. Mrs. Gale was quarantined, and a week later Grandad had to kill her too.

"I don't understand, Grandad. My birds never get stale or wet feed." Monte plied a thumb along his lower lip. "I couldn't bear to tell Mrs. Gale about her bird havin' to be killed."

"I'll tell her." Grandad's fingers brushed the boy's porcupiney hair as softly if it were down, as gently as a leaf deciding autumn had come.

There was worse. They had to kill the mealy's squabs. She had picked them something awful, and one was practically dead from shock.

"Keep her away from the others, but look after her. She's the one will win Murwillumbah for you this year. That's her distance, I reckon. I know her kind; she could win that race for you for a couple of years. Just don't bother mating her again."

"I bloody won't!"

"She's only a bird and doesn't know what makes her go crazy like that."

"Heck, Grandad, I'm havin' some bad luck."

"It comes in bags, Boy. But you've got some younguns there I'd swap my Henry Lawson set for." Grandad's eyes assured the kid this was not merely consoling bullshit. "After-dark's raising a couple of magnificent-looking birds. And the red-checker's settled down . . . and I can hardly believe how Boadicea's littl'n has come on. Tiny, but built like a bloody ark. A real corker."

"Hey, that's what I'll call her." A quick smile husked Monte's mouth of its incipient bitterness. "Corker!"

These spoiled fat ugly gloating young birds reared up when approached, spindle-shanked, angry and fearlessly cawing like stunted offsprings of a fervent Phoenix. In a few months they grew into sleek alert charmers, sudden to remonstrance when either Monte or their mothers annoyed them.

As the year progressed the lives of the wheeling Boomeroosters spun closer and faster around the greatest event since the ending of World War II.

Though Lillipilli Valley was twelve thousand Suez miles from London, Buckingham Palace sometimes seemed only a gibber's hoist from the other side of Mrs. Allsop's back fence. From her kitchen window that lady could probably tell you what color undies the Queen was wearing on a particular day. And for once she was in accord with her countrywomen when she gave the Coronation her excited blessing.

"I'm glad Elizabeth married that Phil'p Mountbatten. 'E's a bonza bloke. I've seen him in the newsreels; goin' down the mines in Wales like dear old Eddy used to, doin' the barn dance in Canada, and larkin' round Paris. And they've got two boska kids. She's a proper Lady and Phil'p's a real Jack Robertson."

In Allsop annals there was never a greater knighthood than to be dubbed a Jack Robertson. It was the pinnacle. The ironbark of the bush. The shaft of the mine. The pint pot of the pub. The scrum of the game.

In Allsop heaven Jack Robertson would be closer to Ben Hall than either Rommel or God. And when Alice Arden Henrietta Allsop said so in her bustier-than-Melba voice . . .

"Well, she has got a better voice than Gracie Fields."

. . . one could imagine Jack Robertson, sword upraised and gilt all over, overwhelming the other political idiots of his day, in the singing silver of his testimonial words: "*Unlock the land.*"

Bless you Henry Allsop for making it known that this man, in his parable of foresight, gave Australia to its people, and freed them of strange chains that until then seemed inviolable.

The Coronation Day sky was gorged on sunlight and June blue, and the holiday became a sublime success, especially when the Boomeroo Bulls defeated the Cucumbers in a raucous morning Rugby Union game. Footballers and followers, already looped on London's lead, got drunker than Anzacs on their day of the year.

Oh, the Boomeroo Bulls are . . .
on the piss again . . . on the . . .
piss again . . .

"Let's know if they're ever off it." There was more froth on that than a Gallipoli donkey could kick over. Some men were even dragged from the bar-enclaves of the pubs for a few hours to share the joy with their families.

"Christ, Mary, we 'ad the kids to keep you company. Can't you leave me 'ere in peace with me mates?"

The Catholic Church Coronation Bazaar was such a

financial tax-free, profit-scudding success it was probably treasonable, and the First Elizabeth would have had Father Barry beheaded.

"How much did we make, Father?"

"Enough to keep the devil away for a while, my dear, but not enough to get us out of purgatory."

The Parents and Citizens Coronation Lunch became so speechy it ended up dinnerless.

"Who asked that know-all bastard to Emcee?"

"Some deaf bastard on a diet."

The Coronation Athletics Meet was so event filled and ran so long it was final-less, because even the sun which had never set on the British Empire could not provide enough daylight for such a mini-marathon Games.

"I won every race I was in, Dad. You shoulda been there to see me go."

"I was helpin' out in the pub, son."

"Your father's always helping out in the hotel, son. He's the one keeps the cash register ringing."

"Even the Methodist minister's wife had a shandy at the sportsground."

"Well, she was bloody luckier than me. I couldn't get near the keg for flies, cattle-dogs and half-pissed kids."

The Primary School Pageant was so patriotically British and so garishly Cecil B. DeMille-vile it was garrulously Australian . . .

"You mean it was fuckin' awful!"

"Wasn't the Infants' Maypole Dance sweet, but? Fancy them remembering all those intricate steps."

"Bloody little drongos. Someone shoulda cut off their feet to make it shorter."

Pauline (I-am-not-related-to-Feet-Feet) Anderson sang long and tirelessly while Sixth Class performed an appropriate Gold Rush Ballet tiresomely.

"Ain't that some kinda poofter dancin'?"

"Yeah. Where the girls are supposed to be fairies and the men *are*."

Pauline, nevertheless . . .

"Never again as far as I'm concerned."

. . . did sing valiantly against the sound of a tinny school orchestra and clompy feet.

> "*A young man left his native shore
> For trade was bad at Home* . . .*"*

"That's England all right."

> "*And when he got to Ballarat
> It put him in a glow* . . .*"*

"They musta been drinkin' Ballarat Bitter even back in those days."

> "*Give me the sound of the windlasses
> And cry: Look out below!"*

"What kinda sorts are windlassies?"

"How should I know, grub? Maybe they're molls with indigestion who fart a lot."

At least Pauline finished the song: Sixth Class never did get to the end of the ballet, because the schoolboy diggers got sick of the poofter dancing and started to tickle the fairies where fairies are evidently most ticklish . . . where they sat on their mushrooms.

Duck Allsop recited "Five Miles from Gundagai" and stuck to traditional reality. His dog not only sat on the tuckerbox but also shit on it. As an encore he began "The Bastard from the Bush":

> "*Would ya bash a man an' rob 'im?
> Asked the Leader of the Push.
> I'd bash a man an' fuck 'im,
> Said the Bastard from the* . . .*"*

At that point Duck got the bum's rush from the organizing Miss Bowen, who reminded him that he was no longer a schoolboy and shouldn't have been there. But Duck was a hero: the first boy to curse aloud in front of teachers since Gutsa Mevinney, at age seven, was kicked out of school. He swore violently at a long-gone teacher, Miss Howell, who was very very English and spoke very very precisely and expected children to be very very silent unless they were asked to stand very very straight and answer one of her very very brittle British questions.

Gutsa told her: "I'm bloodywell friggin' goin' home and ain't never comin' back to this bloodyfriggin' joint." He spoke well for a seven-year-old. "I been here a year now an' all I learnt is how to count upta twenty and sing that bloody Lavender's-friggin'-Blue, Dilly Dilly." He made his blunt point.

"And that is probably more than you'll ever learn for the rest of your life, you very very horrid little boy."

Gutsa never did go back to be verbally expelled. After going sporadically to the Catholic school, he went on to become the alertest cockatoo the Boomeroo SP bookie ever had, and the luckiest damn spinner who ever tossed two pennies at the Bora Bora swy school.

"When I'm tossin' the pennies," Gutsa explained, "I use the same backhand flip me old man useda use to knock me old lady arse-over-'ead an' Stiffer than Mo."

The Pacific Avenue Coronation Garden Party was so gate-crashed it was hingeless. The Coronation Midnight Barbecue on Main Road was a Rabelaisian riot.

"Jesus Christ, what a shindig!"

"Holy Mary . . . a whole bloody beast on the spit."

"Bejesus, what a turnout!"

"Good God! I've never seen anything like it before."

The Boomeroo Bulls were not only well and truly pissed but loving one another so much they seemed to be forever in one of their coracle-like prosexual scrums.

"You ought see the rootin' goin' on down at the bottom of the school playground, but."

For once the stars were otiose, so lit was the town. The crowning bond pervaded this world and there was no alarm when Bandy-Andy danced off into the night (or was it morning) wearing Mrs. Clew-Drummond's diamond tiara. The joyful redeemed knew that Constable Harvey would be at Bandy-Andy's shack earlier than the last home-going possum to retrieve the brilliant old-fashioned hairlooming piece.

Bandy-Andy was the town clown. His legs had been broken when he was two by a bolting horse. Until that day his parents hadn't realized their child was almost deaf. In middle age his only stupidity was that he still spoke in a litany of hard-learnt child words. He had never been hurt by anybody older than six or seven and, like all children, he suffered and enjoyed these sticks-and-stones games.

"Where is it, Andy? Mrs. C-D's tiara?"

"I gave it to Jesus' Muvver."

"Now, cut it out, Andy! Mrs. Drummond's goin' to want it back."

"I did! I did!"

"Oh, my God."

"No, not *God*. To Holy Mary, Muvver-of-God."

"OK. But where is it?"

"In the bwoody church!"

"But whereabouts did you put the bloody thing?"

"On 'er bwoody head, of course! You fink I'm silly?"

The celebrating ebbed for a few hours while people flowed into handy doorways to settle down and listen to the man on the wireless tell about the Coronation bash in London . . . where Queen Salote of Tonga, glittering like lightning, was stealing all the thunder.

"This Salutee . . . she's black, ain't she?"

"She ain't brindle, you dickhead!"

"Me daughter's in London, ya know. She was goin' down Whitehall early to get a good possie."

The Lords and Ladies of England — assured of excellent possies — arrived at the Abbey in their mothproofed robes to sit where the week before they had gone to rehearsals with sandwiches in shoe boxes. The Heads of State from the rest of the world, feeling about at home as an Olympic team from Papua on Mars, mingled with Royals from the rest of Europe.

"All those other Kings and Queens belong in *Alice in Wonderland*."

"Couldn't even make up a decent poker pack."

When news of the conquest of Everest swept over them, a world of grandeur opened the sky for a moment before the shouting ripped the town apart. By this time, clouds like lung tissue were packed around the moon, sound-proofing the heavens.

"Where can they go after Everest?"

"There's always Mt. Isa."

"Billy Hawkes's climbed up everything there, including the gins."

In kitchen fastnesses, crouched around the wireless as if it were a whispering thing, they listened through the gathering hours — their hearts collecting with others across the great brooding continent — waiting to be blessed by a young crowned girl, married to a bonza bloke with two boska kids. And when, much later, she spoke, their thoughts travelled round the world. From atolls of light, across parades of prairie, across veldt, timeless Indian hinterlands, immemorial trans-Tasman fjords and ocean-fettered islands: there didn't seem world enough to hold the compassion this young queen brought about, or space enough to encompass her listeners. They, too, felt coronate and pure and young, and alive to the future: unaware that this ambience of emotions began to die the moment it began to live. This was the finish of another time, the end to a flowering the world would never know again.

"Ain't had a crowd sittin' up all night like this since the Bradman Tests."

"The Poms are OK."

"The Canadians *were* good to our airmen in the war."

"Even the New Zealanders are not bad: they are more bloody British than the British, but!"

"The South Africans are a lot like us."

"Except the bastards are better footballers."

The world isn't big enough to hold so many people so close together for too long, and yet too big to reveal such individual beauty. It's like looking at the stars and expecting to recognize a face on some planet.

"Elizabeth might be the last to ever hold us all in the palm of her hand like this."

"I'm gonna remember today forever, Mum."

"Know what, Greta? I feel like I've been crowned myself today. God Bless that little girl who grew up to be our Queen."

Sleep well, Lilibet Windsor. Mrs. Allsop is watching over you and Jack Robertson. She may be the Mercury of gossip but she's a fair Horatio among guardian angels.

Those meandering home in the wavering morning breeze heard Alex Armourial, high and homesick, singing on his front veranda as he thought of his parents still living on the Isle of Man.

> *"When the summer day is over*
> *And its busy cares have flown,*
> *I sit beneath the starlight*
> *With a weary heart alone.*
> *Then arises like a vision,*
> *Sparkling bright in nature's dream,*
> *My own dear Ellan Vannin*
> *With its green hills by the sea."*

"I don't care where you come from . . . if there are no tears in your eyes when Alex Armourial sings 'Ellan Vannin' there are no tears in your heart."

The kids were the last to disappear from the streets. Even little ones were up all night, dribbling after brothers and sisters, determined to be big kids for a day.

"See the boy on front of our Coronation Souvenir books, Li'l Peterdunny? See . . . he's holding another Coronation Souvenir book in *his* hand. Now see the boy on *that* Coronation Souvenir book . . . is he, too, holding *another* Coronation Souvenir book?"

"It depends on the printer," Jerry said. "Some printers are cleverer than others."

"The Japs once sent a pin to England," Monte said, "and it had the Lord's Prayer printed on the head of it. But . . . the Brits drilled a hole in it and sent it back with a dozen pins inside it and the Lord's Prayer printed on the head of the whole bloody lot."

"Gee," Li'l Peterdunny said: now this did enthrall him. "What did the Japs do then?"

"Heck, Peterdan, how should I know? It's just a story; it ain't a Brick Bradford serial."

"Maybe they shoved them up their Emperor's arsehole," Gloamy said.

"Well, we wouldn't do that to *our* Queen," Li'l Peterdunny said, hugging his Coronation Souvenir book and marching off like a Knight with his Garter showing.

And the British Empire was dead.

10

Red-checker had surprised Monte after he moved her downstairs by becoming a very protective parent, and her squeakers bloomed. One was a strange coloring — plumbeous with a tangerine bar. In some light refracted by galvanized iron wire netting he saw a touch of mosaic-pied in her spruce tail.

"She's a bewdy, Grandad," he said. "I think I'll give *her* a name. 'Beauty'!"

"You mean 'Bewdy,'" Grandad said.

After-dark's younguns were both blue-bars like herself, a cock and a hen. He called the hen Mrs. Allsop because she was bossy, always breasting up to her brother and nagging her mother.

Corker feathered a perfect blue-check without a deviation and started coming home fast and regular in the short early flys. Although the official season started uneventfully for Monte it became successful and disastrous in a single weekend. He sent the mealy hen, After-dark, his blue-bar cock champion and Boadicea to Murwillumbah and the mealy won as Grandad had predicted. After-dark and the blue-bar cock were home ten minutes later, but Boadicea was not with them.

Grandad took over the watch while Monte rode his pushbike to Chadla with the mealy hen's ring registered in the pigeon clock. Boadicea was still not home when he returned, so he waited up for her, late into a rather magic but starless and cloudless night, his heart a rubber hammer. Even a boy could feel the purity of this moon-paved sky. Bleached as rime, the moon stayed with him, and long flags of white night gentled the unbroken line of treetops in the school playground, tucking the bedded valley in.

At midnight Grandad called softly. "It's a cold night, Boy. Come to bed. She's probably treed down for the night."

"Soon, Grandad. Boadicea wouldn't straggle." His voice was unerringly stubborn yet calm. "You go back to bed, Grandad . . . please."

"All right. Good night, son."

" 'Night, Gran'ad."

No sympathy can hold or share boy-suffering; it is alien to men and women and perhaps only a dog can come close to being a part of it. The passing hours changed the face of the night, shadowed the eyelid of the moon, and began to apply early morning rouge to the horizon.

At six o'clock Monte spotted a single cloud hiking up the valley on a fast-risen wind — moving faster than a milkman, slower than a paper boy. At first it looked like a flattened ball of cotton, but as it approached it presented more shape. He gammoned to grab it as it scudded nearer but it scrubbed his upraised hands and went on. "Come back here, cloud!"

The configuration of it caught his fancy and chilled his spine when it turned shape as if to the sound of his voice. It pranced like two huge horses: they were drawing some sort of cart. Shaking their manes, they slipped closer to the moon and their silvered shapes revealed they were being driven by a woman in flowing, cloudy robes. She charged her steeds into the plaque of the moon and for the moment became molded there. A goddess . . . in a chariot? A Queen! It was Boadicea. A stalk of dawn, blasted from out of the east, hit the moon and the image — carved and cornelian in the blue vault — was stung upon the boy's memory. His eye conceived it and his mind filed it, preparing his heart to feed on it.

He said aloud to himself, "You're not often wrong, Boy, but you're right again!" Laddering down almost lightheartedly, he looked back over his shoulder and smiled at the disappearing, dissolving cloud. "Thanks, cloud. Give my love to Mrs. Kafoots."

He went into the house and slept the kind of sleep theologians dream about while tossing and turning in their hammocks. He slept with a faith that had nothing to do with the consuming proportions of religion, and with a dreaming concentration that comes from unrestricted bargaining with all and any listening gods.

"Gee I slept well, Grandad."

"Boy . . . you have been asleep for a bit over twenty-four hours," Grandad said. "I figured I'd bury you if you didn't wake up for your porridge this morning."

"You mean I've slept a whole day of my life away?"

"At your age! How could you afford it?"

"Would you've buried me pigeon clock with me?" Monte groped for his breakfast chair.

"No. Just those damn paintbrushes."

"*Grandad!*"

"You won the Murwillumbah Fly."

They looked at each other with bald-faced concentration and said simultaneously, in well-metered meaning: "I told you so."

"Mr. Hadford dropped by to tell me." The old man eased both boy and chair closer to the table. He touched the back of the boy's shirt collar where it was frayed, his eyes filled with all the words love and emotion can give birth to at the drop of a tear.

"Grandad . . . Boadicea . . . di'n't come home."

"I know." Grandad's tongue was embossed with feelings incubated in man for a million years: sometimes the voice seems an unnecessary evolution.

"Growin' up ain't easy," Monte said. "I'll be glad when it's over."

The old man went to his own chair and they started to eat their oats — which now swam in melted brown sugar — in silent agreement. The clock chimed, warning them of time. "Don't be scared of the few years you spend growing physically, Richard. They're not many really."

"I'm not afraid, Grandad. Just . . . impatient, I guess."

"Well, remember . . . no matter what happens, I'm on your side. Today, tomorrow and as long as I'm here. No matter what! You come to me and I'll listen to you and understand. Too many people get lost before they are old enough to start looking for life. That's not going to happen to you. Understand?"

"Yes, Grandad. I just feel a bit frazzled."

The youngster sounded unhappy but he felt good. It was beaut to know what had always been there always would be. He felt imperial.

It became apparent that Corker was a pigeon to watch.

Young as the blue-checker was, she was never far behind her older, conditioned and more experienced loft relatives. Trapping in well, giving up her ring without one antic of a flutter, never quibbling with the other birds about any necessary pigeon hole, Corker guaranteed Monte those precious minutes that often seesawed between victory and defeat once a bird was actually home.

Bewdy was fast but temperamental and took to boy-watching from Garsides' chimney, teasing Monte from there and sometimes taking up to twenty minutes to trap in.

Mrs. Allsop and her blue-bar brother travelled well together in good times, but after they ducketed she would chase him from niche to niche, henpecking him while Monte tried to collar them and collect their rings.

Corker may have sensed his desperation after her mother Boadicea was lost, because she won the Armidale Fly in astounding time, then went on to take everything before her.

"My blue-checker Corker won the Tenterfield in record time, Mr. Carney."

"Euchred 'em, eh?"

"Corker won the Lismore Fly, Gutsa, you old bastard. Whatya thinka that?"

"Let me know when she comes home from Woop Woop, kid . . . they eat pigeons there."

Monte ran into Goldie in Kincomba one afternoon after school.

"Did you know that a man drove all the way down from Murrurundi to buy my blue-checker Corker, Miss Killorn?"

"You didn't sell her?" Goldie held her expected breath.

"Not on your bloo . . . oomin' life!"

"Must be an extraordinary bird," Goldie said. "Would you like a friend of mine to give Corker a mention in the newspaper next weekend?"

"Could you arrange *that*?"

"With a little . . ." Goldie scratched the air with a little finger. "Besides, I owe you one for the egg display. Which reminds me . . ." She scuffed his hair. "I've been carrying this around for absolute months. Hardly ever get to Boomeroo these days. Here!" She handed him a folded envelope from her crocodile handbag. "It's an order on Duxmann Bros. for a watch. To the value of thirty pounds. You'll get a very good one for twenty-nine."

"Struth . . . this'll take the wind out of Grandad's sails." Monte's mouth was open wider than for a dentist. "But you . . ."

"If you are going to say I shouldn't have I'll bash you, Boy Howard," Goldie said tomboyishly, vibrantly smiling and exhibiting a fist. "That display is still being talked about." She didn't add that it also included several thousand pounds' worth of stuffed birds.

"I'll keep this watch when I get it till the day I die."

"Don't do that," she said softly. "Just until the day you can afford to buy a better one, or until someone who loves you gives you another. You're a nice boy . . . Boy." She bent down and kissed him in the middle of Kincomba, among all those scurrying shoppers, and he didn't feel the least bit embarrassed.

How did such sincere boys grow into insincere galoots? Goldie wondered, thinking of Ben Leslie.

The kids took over Corker's fame and made her a schoolhold word.

"Betya Howdie's Corker will win the Coolangatta Cup next Saturday."

"She'll piddle in."

"A cove from Warialda offered Monte fifty quid for Corker."

"My Uncle Dray from Wallabadah would pay him a hundred pound, I bet."

"Your uncle from Wallabadah's only good for burpin' like the turkeys he keeps."

"Corker'll soon be worth more than that there colt from Old Regret."

If egging on created winners, it was becoming impossible for Corker to lose. The mealy hen and red-checker began to lag when the flys went inter-State, so Monte pulled them out for the rest of the season. The blue cocks,

After-dark, Mrs. Allsop and Bewdy were still flying consistently well; so he now had a sensible idea of which birds were capable of flying the best times from various distances across the Queensland border. From Charleville, Gympie, Maryborough, Rockhampton, Longreach, Mingary: towns with years of fascination behind their faraway meanings. Bewdy beat Corker home from Charleville, but fooled and fluttered around Garsides' chimney so long that Corker, trapping in seven minutes later, still won.

"Bewdy musta hitchhiked with Ansett."

"She bloodywell must believe in Santa Claus the way she hangs round that chimley . . ."

"Chimney, Grandad," Monte said.

Grandad thrust the pigeon clock at him. He now believed Bewdy was not worth training.

A Grand Coronation Year Fly had been planned by the Sydney, Newcastle and Lillipilli clubs for September, June having been too early in the year for a worthwhile race. It had been calculated that the Newcastle birds would fly from Rockhampton, high on the shank of the Queensland coast, the Lillipilli birds from Marlborough to the north and the Sydney flocks from Eubobo, south of Rockhampton. Distance variations and time allowances were to be worked out by a combined committee. Monte entered five birds but no yearling, since he believed it was just too early for his young ones.

A Sydney newspaper gave the Coronation Fly a mention one Saturday on a back sports page buried beneath the usual stableful of horse-racing shit, and a Newcastle paper printed a short, bone-detailed column on it beneath the horses, beside the dogs and above the badminton. When Goldie Killorn's enterprising friend on the *Kincomba Compass* discovered Corker had never recently been beaten he did some homework and found that the kid who owned this unbeatable bird wasn't even entering it in the Coronation Fly.

A week later Monte found himself on the back page of the *Compass* beside a blank space. General Neguib was on the front page, a stuffed pigeon superimposed on his shoulder.

"Aw, that Neguib's a bit of a statue, an' any pigeon would love to shit on that uniform."

"Some of those rich Wops got strange migrating habits. They take off for Switzerland after shittin' in their own nests and never go back."

"My Dad says that Gyppo oughta be stuffed instead of the pigeon," Duck said, and copped a mouthful of knuckles from young Ibbi Sutti.

A woman with a lot of wires . . .

"Loose."

. . . and two electricians with a truck . . .

"With a sick cylinder head."

. . . who called herself Happee O'Day and said she represented 2KC Kincomba, arrived unannounced to *do* Monte for the 2KC Happee Hour. She talked like a funny-farmer and laughed like a woodpecker isolated in a steel foundry.

"Here we are again, Happees. Today we are visiting Monte Howard in Boomeroo. You're a boy and you go to High School and you're only twelve, aren't you, Monte?" Big Happee shuffled unhappily among the humbugging kids who gathered like hopeful chihuahuas around a big unreachable slut.

"I'm thirteen," Monte said.

"Our listeners on 2KC . . ."

"Two Keen Cunts," Duck Allsop yelled, dodging an electrician who poked him with something like a prodding stick.

". . . want to know all about you and your famous pigeon," Happee said. "Oh my!"

Duck was now perched on Kyle's fence and dating her up: Feet-Feet came along and grounded him in one foul whoop.

"Now, Monte, I believe your little Corker has never been beaten," Happee suggested.

"He beats it regularly," Duck shouted, whipping away from Feet-Feet. "But not his bird."

"Not in a long fly," Monte said. "She's a blue-checker..."

"CORKER," all the kids chorused.

"When did you first become interested in racing pigeons, Monte? Speak up, now! All our Happee Hour listeners want to hear about you and Corker."

"I can't remember."

"Hahahahaha... did you hear that Happees? He can't remember."

"Since I was born, I guess," Monte said.

"My dear, how do you mean?"

"My Grandad flew them. They were here before me."

"I see! It's a family tradition. Isn't that sweet? A big cheer for Monte, boys and girls." Big Happee was rolling into it and the kids cheered like a mob of tumbling idiots.

"Booooooooooh-booooooo." Dissenting Duck.

"And where is your dear old granddaddy now, Monte?" Happee sounded as if the answer should be in heaven or Happyland.

"He's inside, but he won't come out. He doesn't go for crap... and he ain't old."

Big Happee gave one of the technicians a glance and his nod assured her that he had caught the "crap." She heaved up her breasts and her eyes skirted the women now arranged along the Kyle and Gale fences. "Hahahahaha... You're a lucky boy to have such a dear old grandfather to have given you an interest in your sweet little pidgies."

The "pidgies" did it! Monte had stomached the earlier

"granddaddy" because he knew he and Grandad would get a laugh from that later but . . . "pidgies"?

"It's got nothing to do with luck, lady," Monte said quite loudly. "It's breeding and training and general care that count. More things can go wrong than you can shake a snake at if you're not careful. Some of my birds have blood strains developed over forty years . . . more! Just because I don't have a lot of pigeons don't mean they haven't got pedigrees."

"*Doesn't* mean . . ." Elizabeth Griffith called out and Monte stared her out of the front ranks, thinking: Bejesus, the whole bloody town's here.

"Of course not, darling," Happee said in her throatiest theatrical voice. "My, my! He does take his pidgies seriously, doesn't he, Happees? And rightly so! We should all care for our pets."

"They're not pets, missus," Monte said.

"Isn't it wonderful to meet such an ardent young person?" Big Happee kept pressing her mike between her blossoming breasts between bursts. "I hope all you children at home have your Happee pads out, jotting down your score for Monte, to give him a chance to win the Big Happee Badge at the end of the year."

She flung her fingers up the back of her neck and careered her hair defiantly at the fence gallery. "Now, Monte, tell us why you haven't entered Corker in the Coronation Fly."

"It's too much yet for my first-season birds," Monte said. "In another month maybe . . . I gotta go now." It was getting harder to remain polite. "It's time to train my birds, so I gotta scoot all these kids out of the yard."

"Hahahahaha . . . isn't he the young devil? All right, darling, Happee will forgive you for such a good reason."

"With such a good reason for such a good purpose," Elizabeth said, game again and sidling closer.

Big Happee gave her a wash-day look she no doubt wished had been a broom handle; then, after cherishing her breast with the mike again, said to Monte, "Say something to the Happee Clubbers before you go, Monte dear." Her mike was still very close to her breast when she presented it to him and the white flesh almost blanked out his entire vision.

For a moment he marvelled at the vastness of the two toe-size teats boggling him, then he stuttered, "Goo' bye."

"Hey, Happee! Hey, lady! My name's Duck Allsop and I got this dirty black retriever what does tricks."

"Go away, you snotty little brute," Happee said.

"Well, git stuffed, ya long-nosed pain," Duck said. "An' I know why Grandad locked himself inside. I heard him say you was a silly coot." Duck goosed her as she tried to sidestep him.

"Oh . . . hahahahaha . . . ah . . . ohhhh!" Happee forgot her staircase-wit repertoire and ran for the truck, which was a more sensible maneuver than fronting Duck-cum-drake. The 2KC Happee Van took off through a swirl of kids and an eddy of resounding cheers, which is what Happee had come to achieve.

"Bloody little brats," she said to the technicians. "Why do I do it? I could make more in Chadla on a Saturday night letting weirdos photograph my boobs than I make in a fortnight at 2KC."

"Because you're hopelessly moral, Gwennie," one of them said.

And Gwennie herself had learnt long ago that the world was conventionally astigmatic: it did not like moral people to look anything but; it liked to be able to pinpoint a person's immorality. The world didn't know the half of it.

11

IT WAS NOT SURPRISING that a Kincomba patriot of Councillor Duxmann's dimensions should take it upon his Pickwickian shoulders and belly to right this nonsense about Corker not flying in the Coronation Fly and winning glory for Kin . . . the Lillipilli Valley: "It's like not entering Phar Lap in the Melbourne Cup."

"It's none of his bleedin' business."

"That fat dickhead is only interested in business that's none of his business."

In his Chambers the ponderous Councillor said, "Pooh-pooh! A boy of that age doesn't know what's best for himself, let alone a pigeon he probably pinched from the Kincomba Domain in the first place."

"I believe it's a well-bred bird, sir," a well-meaning servant said.

"I said pooh-pooh," Duxmann Pooh Bah said.

"Here are some recent clippings about this and other pigeons you may like to peruse, sir," the aide added.

"Shut up and get my car!" This was meant to be Caesar upon hearing that Pompey was on the Appian Way, but it sounded more like Goldwyn or Mayer on being told

Shakespeare was on his way to Hollywood. "I'll ride roughshod over that larrikin."

This was the Saturday before the mid-week Coronation Fly, and during that afternoon, while Monte was waiting for his birds to come home from a long Queensland Fly, the Duxmann Buick drew up in front of the flower-pot ochre house on Harrow Street. Damon Quentin Duxmann, civic politician-cum-louder, a man with a red-carpet mind, a shifty nature, a bone-lazy body, a large throat and little else except the push that came with it — a man to make Jack Robertson and Ben Hall puke — backed out of the bribery-won Buick.

Grandad was at Bill Swanton's playing chess; but Damon Quentin hammered loudly enough to disturb Vonnie Kyle, who was barracking on a loser at Randwick ridden by a midget maniac who had . . . "made his bloody run twice; too soon and then too late. Little bugger ought to be throttled with his own jockstrap!"

Mrs. Kyle came to the side gate to see who was trying to wake the doornail. She seemed amazed to see the Councillor, but certainly recognized him. She looked at her watch as if to question the sun.

"The old man's down at Swanton's. The kid's sure to be in his ducket. *If* you're knocking at the right back door."

"Ducket?" Damon had knowledge of only two words sounding like that: bucket and the other one.

"Pigeon ducket." Vonnie's thumb did the rest.

"Oh, indeed." Without a thank-you, the self-blessed pride of Kincomba went thataway. At the foot of the ladder-stairway he called: "Are you up there, sonny?"

Monte was suspicious because of the "sonny." "Who dat?" He sounded not unlike Hattie McDaniel, surprised, in a comedy of terrors.

"Who-dat?"

"Who-dat say who-dat?"

"Who-dat say who-dat when I say who-dat?"

He went to the upstairs lookout and peered down upon the political bod, whom he recognized as the fatso who had given a thin, starving speech one lunchtime to the new High School students at the beginning of the year . . .
"Young men! Kincomba is now your world: there is much here for you to absorb."
"Looks like he ate it all before we got 'ere."
"Too many cucumbers make me fart."
Smiling in recollection, Monte managed a polite, "Sir?"
"I hear you're not entering your best bird in the Coronation Flight?" The huff-and-puff man came to the point before blowing the ducket down. After all, he was a pointless politician and, like all his comrades in qualms, knew that when you had no sharp argument the harder-faster you made them sit on it the better your chance of getting results.
"Fly, sir. It's called a fly."
"That is interesting." D.Q. was at his oily, if not beastly, best. "Your decision seems selfish . . . some might say?"
"Well, you see, sir . . . my blue-checker Corker is still pretty young and . . ."
"Don't hedge . . ." What a magnificent turnaround for the shire's number one word-gardener! ". . . I've read up on pigeons and know that their first year is very often their best. By the way, are you coming down or shall I come up?"
Surveying that proposition, Monte decided he had no choice. Blind Freddie could see that the Councillor was no Edmund Hillary.
The boy came out and climbed down. "I'll come down; I know the ropes."
"Look, lad! Your bird is a champion! We all agree on that. The world needs leaders and your pigeon is a leader among birds."
Used to the reasoning of a Kate Cruikshank, Monte

couldn't accept such phony diplomacy, not to mention that barrage of body. "But I already have the limit of five birds entered, sir."

"Mere formality." The fatty waved his arms above the boy's head as though blessing the flatulence in the air around him. "There are firms in Kincomba will donate goodly prizes if the Coronation winner is from . . . hereabouts."

(" 'Goodly'? Miss Cruikshank?")

"And I mean goodly prizes," Duxmann reiterated with a Mass of meaning.

"A new pigeon clock?" Monte spoke before he had control of his pride, and the man had him.

"Yes. Yes, indeed," Duxmann said, hooking his voice and putting his baited hands on his quarry's shoulders. "A new pigeon clock." Now he was blessing the boy in the soft tones kept for kissing babies. "You enter this bird of yours in the Coronation Fli . . . Fly . . . and I personally guarantee you, win or lose, lad, win or lose, a bright new shining, priceless pigeon clock. Bring it to you myself to clock the winner home. Isn't that what they're for? What do you say to that, young-fellow-me-lad?"

A young fellow knows many things, among them the fact that he *is* only a lad who lives in an adult world. He may have pride and principle in his makeup, but he knows that the costly material things are beyond him. And what is greed when the chips are thrown in for you, the dice are loaded in your favor, and everything on the felt is made reachable?

Monte had no doubts that Corker could win. He finally said, "All right, Mr. Duxmann." Only having to say the words was throttling. "What about another ring number, but?"

"Formality," Mephisto-mouth said. "Don't worry about another thing. I'll fix it . . . up. You just send your little feathered friend along instead of one of the other birds and leave the rest to me and I'll . . ."

Duxmann cocked his chin: it wasn't easy. Some raving Rachmaninoff was composing on the horn of his car. "Who would dare do that?"

Monte shrugged. He knew who would not only dare but who would do it and be damned. His listening innocence was unglazed.

"Leave the arrangements to me . . . simply make sure that bird wins." Full of Duxmania, the Councillor dolly-stepped off as fast as his paddle-feet could perform.

Duck met Damon on the battlefield of the street with a tongue to match the shire shyster's. "Give us a lift round the block in ya Buick, mister."

"Go home, if you have one, you dirty urchin, before I call the police."

Duck extended his arm to include some gathered kids. "We ain't never had a ride in a posh car."

"Nor a wash, I should say," Damon said.

"Yer a mean old bastard," Duck said.

Chafing, wishing he had commandeered a chauffeur, D.Q. almost stuttered, "How . . . dare you speak to me in that manner?"

"An' you've got them bulgin' balls like Old Tuggeroo Mac's. You kin 'ardly walk, lest run!"

"I'll have you put so far away your own lice will never find you," Duxmann threatened.

"Yeah, and then I'll yell for the police and tell 'em you got me in the back of the Buick an' tried to bum-fuck me . . . and made me lick ya dirty dick." Duck lay down in front of the limousine and began screaming. "Help, help! 'E's got me by the prick!" He then stood up calmly and said, "After that you'll be the one locked up, you Cucumber cunt."

"Oh, my God, let me get out of this place."

Soon after, Jerry scampered up into the ducket. "You should've heard Duck, Mont. He was worse than I've ever heard him before. I wonder if he's goin' off his rocker?"

"Did Duxmann do his loll?" Monte's guilt feelings wanted revenge.

"Oh, yes! When he got into the Buick and it wouldn't start he called Duck for everything over the moon; but then Duck just sauntered off." Jerry listed on his haunches. "Angela had a look and found the distributor cap was gone . . . or something like that. She's gone up to Allsops' now. *He's* in our place." Jerry's eyes darted across Monte's frown.

"Sounds shoofty to me," Monte said: "Does your Mum know him?"

"Seems that way."

Monte buried the brief silence. "I'm sending Corker in the Coronation basket when she comes home today."

"Did he talk you into it?"

"Sort of." It was a nick of admission.

"You didn't want to send her."

"What's that matter now? I am. Do you want to help me catch the other birds for the Corro basket or not?"

"Of course."

"Don' worry about the mosiac-pied."

After selecting the remaining nominated birds Monte said, "Corker should be home by now."

"You're taking her for granted," Jerry said.

"And you sound shitty! Ain't my fault your Mum's stuck with that old bugger. I didn't ask him to come to Boomeroo."

There are times when friendship can blow-dry your heart like an impassioned willy-willy; when your conscience pinches you like a fierce little mud-crawtchie. You can't evade the issue as you would a dust storm or a snapping yabbie. And if you feel your friend is right and you are wrong it hurts like nettled hell. Even shaking your head evasively stings.

"If only it was a few weeks later . . . you said," Jerry said.

"Look! I don't give a wombat's piss about that fat galoot from Kincomba," Monte said. "I know Corker can win. Her Gympie time's a State record already. So why shouldn't I let her prove that she's the best there is? She is! And I own her."

"The whole world knows that," Jerry said.

"Funneeeeeee-bunny."

"I hope you're never sorry," Jerry said.

"That sounds like a whammy if ever I heard one. Are you still going to give Grandad a hand down to the station with the basket if I'm not back in time?"

"Of course I am!" Jerry gollopped emotional phlegm. "But I hope she's late home today . . . oh, no I don't! Just guess I wouldn't be able to do it if she was mine." Jerry only had one other world apart from Monte: the universe of his school books. Not much boyhood there: it wasn't easy to breathe in those endless pages.

"You could hope she wins."

"All right, I hope."

They shared grim grins, but their doubts were facial. Like two small animals grazing on some mental veldt, aware of a lion called life, but instinctively hungry.

The Ten-bob Angel didn't get a very warm or heavenly reception at Allsops', because she interrupted that lady's favorite radio serial, "Those Feveral Girls."

"After all, Thelma, 'Those Feveral Girls' is the only decent thing you can switch to on a Saturday afternoon when you've done your dough on the horses. It reminds me of one of those three-hanky movies of the thirties when the lovers were always living a lifetime in a day. My . . .

when Ann Harding and Irene Dunne loved a man — especially if it was John Boles — he knew it and was always willing to suffer as much as they did . . . and watch out Genevieve Tobin or Glenda Farrell if they got into the wrong bedroom."

"But Those Feveral Girls do all their living at night."

"Well, that's the way the sheet's folded these days." Nobody could ever say Mrs. Allsop wasn't a product of evolutionary melodrama.

"Where *is* Duck now, Mrs. Allsop?" The Ten-bob Angel asked pleasantly, not wishing to upset the town's common adversary.

"Duuuuuck!" Only human mothers can raise their voices in that unbelievably canine-high pitch when summoning their young. It seems deliberately tuned so that the offspring will not know whether the caller or the called is in danger. Animals and birds are much more honest and more maternally basic.

When Aldertons' chickens heard that commotion they thought chook Doomsday had come and caught them with their combs down, and answered Mrs. Allsop in a loud display of fowl pandemonium.

"Whattayawant, Muuuuuuum?"

"Come'ere!"

Meanwhile, Mr. Alderton came to his back door with a loaded shotgun, the empty hope in his mind that the glad day had arrived when he might catch that dirty big black retriever in his chicken house, red-legged, with blood in its teeth and henshit in its tail.

"Where is it, Duck? The distributor cap?" the Ten-bob Angel asked sweetly when Duck ambled bumptiously out of the tool shed.

"Whatya mean, Angela?" Innocence was never so raped as when on Duck's face. For a boy so well known to defeat — and humiliation and everlasting turmoil — it was a wonder he never mastered the slightest semblance of sinlessness.

"I told you," Mrs. Allsop said. "Duck's never been as light-fingered since his Uncle Frank caught him at his bike-shop till and stuck his hands in the dunny can." Duck was now looking as ecstatic as a blowfly sounded in an unflushed shithouse.

Looking at the shed from which Duck had so shooftily (too-cocksuredly) materialized, Angela asked, "May I take a look?"

"Sure, but hurry up," Mrs. Allsop said. "I gotta get tea ready before the old man gets home from the two-up."

"Won't be a moment," Angela said, and reappeared in less time than that.

Duck was ready, but so was his Mum. Duck jumped at the same time as Mr. Alderton decided to air his shotgun just in case that dirty big black retriever was lurking out there somewhere in the wonderworld of chicken coops. As though warned by a starter's gun, the quick-thinking Alice Arden Henrietta, with stopwatch alertness, stuck out her left foot and tripped her hurtling son. As he sprawled in front of her she grabbed the millet broom — which was used to hold back the gauze door that Reggie Allsop was fond of putting his drink-leaden foot through — and began whaling into the boy, one heel now on his neck. Mrs. Allsop was expert at swinging this broom by the millet end, giving the four-foot broom handle great bounce and power. A rhythm of rage.

The Ten-bob Angel, waving something that looked like a black rubber octopus, nodded and marched past in step to the vroom of the broom.

Duck would have suffocated except his face was buried in the wet airy softness of buffalo grass which grew in a disgustingly wild mattress around the undrained area of the back door.

"You'll have me in my grave before I'm a Granma," his mother wailed. Duck being an only child, she was flaying him dangerously close to the tender machinery of his body which was most likely some day to promote her to that longed-for granniedom she belted on about.

Deep in the buffalo grass Duck's voice was fervently babbling remembered Latin from the few irregular Masses he hadn't sneaked out of. An eavesdropping Spanish Inquisitor would probably have sold his soul to the next heretic in the fire queue just to have heard such fulfilling confessional regret.

When Corker trapped in Monte put her ring in the hatch of the pigeon clock, moistened her mouth, put on a new ring, then settled her down in the Coronation Fly basket. If Jerry hadn't been there he would have cuddled her for the first time. Corker looked at him, blinking her eyes like a couple of camera shutters gone beserk and shaking her head eccentrically, as if she sensed his temptation.

"Won't she be hungry?" Jerry said.

"She'll be fed on the way. They don't expect anything as soon as they're home."

"They don't expect to get shipped off again, either."

"We ain't goin' over all that again."

Grandad was home, so Monte took his pushbike out of the washhouse. "I'll take the clock to Chadla now. Grandad. I might be back in time, but if I'm not, Jerry's goin'ta give you a hand down to the station with the basket."

Grandad seemed anchored in the kitchen doorway, and merely said, "All right, Boy." He, too, sensed the presence of temptation and guilt. He had heard of Duxmann's visit.

All the way to Chadla Monte asked himself why he hadn't told Grandad he had swapped Corker over for the mosaic-pied. Motives had never been surface or sediment to his thinking processes before this, so he was in a foreign state. He did not feel proud.

When he pedalled home an hour and a half later Grandad and Jerry had gone. Riding frantically to the railway station, he free-wheeled up the ramp of the goods platform, but the Express was pulling out. He hung over the white paling fence watching the receding train wordlessly, his heart stabbing him more sharply than the picket fence palings pierced his rib cage. Before the guard's van rounded out of view he whispered, " 'Bye Corker ... give my love to ... Mrs. ... Kafoo ..." Was that a tear?

"Well?" Jerry said when Monte met the two basketeers in the waiting room.

Monte ignored him and said to his grandfather, "Did Jerry tell you I decided to send Corker?"

"No. I saw her when I checked the crate. Why? Did you want Jerry to tell me, Boy?" The old man could go no farther. He stepped back and drew two imaginary guns, as he and Monte often did to each other in mock aggression. Monte didn't have the nous to answer that action truthfully ... or he didn't know the answer. Unable to add to the kid's anxiety, Grandad holstered his phantom guns and said, "She'll make it. She mightn't win but she'll make it. And ... she just might win!"

"Oh, Grandad."

"Hey ... come on, Richard ... she'll be OK. She'll be home before you can say Stinking Biddy Springs."

Jerry remained silently disapproving ... and jealous of the old arms that enfolded his mate.

"Look," Grandad said blusteringly, "I never hardly get over to this side of town. While I'm here I might's well have a schooner at the Railway pub. See a few old cronies. I won't be long." He gave Monte the caress of a grin. "You go home and put some veggies on."

Monte acknowledged the trust and spun his bike round

madly in the empty waiting room. "Come on, Kylie! I'll doubleya home if you're game. You stay and have a few beers with your mates, Grandad. No rush. Me an' Jerr'll cook tea fit for a king."

They fantailed the bike home recklessly through the outgoing Saturday evening traffic, unnerving the meek and irritating the brave. Monte jumped off puffing. "You're getting heavy, Jerry. I won't be able to double you round much longer."

"There's a lot of things we won't be able to do much longer," Jerry said, touching Monte's shoulder fragilely.

"Corker came home in record time today," Monte said evasively. "It'll be in next month's *Pigeon Gazette*. She really is a champ, you know, Jerry."

"Exactly," Jerry said impudently. "I am glad for you." He accorded this as an apology. Squinting in the last battlement of sunlight cast over the back yard, standing like a young Icarus ready to take off, he looked triumphantly magnetic, if not as masculinely handsome as Swiftie Madison. His fair hair shone in the fading light, juggling it in the same way as the shimmering leaves of a camphor laurel did.

"Come in and play cards tonight," Monte said, as they carved potatoes and sculptured pumpkin.

"I'm not very good at cards."

"No one else will be here except Grandad. I won't see much of Gloamy and Batter till the footie's finished; and Swiftie's gone to Chadla for the weekend to stay with a kid from Tech . . . he says. If you ask me I think he's trying to latch on to some sheila over there."

Too many things were passing too fast. The simplicity of life was going down the drain.

"Swiftie's pretty flush with money these days, isn't he?" Jerry said.

"I've noticed," Monte said. It was something he hadn't

wanted to contemplate. "I am stuck on my physics, by the way."

"The awful truth!" Jerry said and for once laughed loudly. "All right. I'm not doing all-fire hot on history. Maybe after we sort each other out we can play casino. I I can handle that."

"Goodio. You get some lolly-water from Feet-Feet and we'll sneak a bit of rum into it," Monte said. "And I've got a shilling so we'll get a packet of Cavaliers. I wanta learn to do the drawback better than Swiftie."

"I can pinch a couple of cigars," Jerry said and they grinned at each other, now with onion tears in their eyes.

"Ask your Mum if you can sleep here," Monte said, a frosting of innocence in his usually clear eyes.

"Should I?"

"You'd like to, wouldn't you?"

"Of course!"

"Well?"

"You sound as stubborn as I did down at the station," Jerry said. "I better get inside then, and have a bath *now*. That place gets busy early on a Saturday night.

"You don't have to have a wash."

"I want to."

"Well, I ain't botherin'."

Jerry smiled adultly, shook his head wisely and said softly, "That doesn't matter."

"OK. You rush, and I'll finish gettin' the tea."

"I won't be long."

"Ooroo for now."

They sounded like two Boy Scouts who'd started a bushfire instead of a camp fire. Their bodies were talking a language their minds preferred not to listen to.

12

For the next few days Monte listened regularly and earnestly to the man on the wireless giving the local, State and National News so that he wouldn't miss any of the weather reports.

The man on the wireless was kept busier than usual, because it seemed there were lots of important things going on in the busy world — which cared nothing about the Coronation Fly. General Neguib wanted to control the Suez Canal. The Shah was back in Persia again . . . and a man thought to have been *torn to pieces* by the *celebrating* Teheran mob a few weeks before was now known to be alive.

"I wonder who sewed him up?"

"Them wogs are good tailors!"

"That must be all they're fuckin' good for."

Meanwhile, back at the wireless station, the man, who was very straightlaced . . .

"You mean straight-stitched?"

. . . continued enlightening a darkening world.

"He shoulda been around in them Dark Ages. He loves to let you know if it looks like the world's comin' to an end."

"They reckon the world will come to an end."

"Everything comes to an end except the queue outside a Chadla brothel on a Saturdee night, grub."

"Yeah, soldiers up soldiers before they even get to the bloody door."

"They only git about three minutes with the whore."

"I'd rather flog meself."

"You got no other choice, Pinhead."

"They useda flog themselves in the Dark Ages."

"Hell, men have been floggin' themselves since Eve appled-off with the bloody snake."

"You reckon Adam whopped himself?"

"Shitabrick, how would I know? Ain't you got any imagination yourself?"

"Sure you 'ave, 'aven'tya, Billy? Just can imagine anybody else havin' a go at your missus while you're away chasing black velvet in Mt. Isa, canya?"

In a Boomeroo pub your province of mind doesn't have to be in the country of the crotch, but if it is you're no foreigner. There's always a welcome in the valley of the thighs.

The man on the wireless often attributed quotes to a Mr. Funny-so-and-so in America, who was called a Radio Announcer, evidently famous there for his unfunny sayings.

"President Auriole of France is considering asking Mistinguette, Colette and Josephine Baker to form yet another Coalition Government."

"Bejesus, I didn't know they were short of coal in France."

"Malenkov's present theme song is 'Georgia on My Mind.'"

"You know, Clarice, those Russians are getting to be more Americanized than us ... raising turkeys in Wallabadah, now, we are! Soon they'll be askin' us to eat more hamburgers than meat pies."

Eventually and happily the man on the wireless quit quoting Mr. Funny-so-and-so and got down to weather tacks instead of tacky jokes. "Showers but bright long intervals . . . so sorry, long bright intervals for most of the north coastal areas. Dry inland with occasional winds coming up later from the sea."

"It's always dry fuckin' inland . . . it's a great bloody desert!"

"A dry-fuck's better'n no fuck, just the same."

"Hey, Big Grub's gotta sense of humor."

"Which is more'n he's ever got in his pocket."

Immediately after Monte had sighed relief, that double-crossing bugger on the wireless coughed . . . twice . . .

"Just like he was havin' an Army medical in one of Errol's war pictures and the doctor was holdin' his balls."

"Cor . . . fancy having Errol Flynn's balls in ya hand . . ." There'd be three minutes' silence in the ladies' lounge for that one.

Then the wireless man added, "So sorry. We have just received a late report of early bushfires on the Queensland border, along the heavily timbered slopes of the McPherson Range near . . . Canungra . . . Police suspect . . ."

"What else?"

"Oh, no . . . Did you hear that, Grandad? Bushfires on the border!"

"It mightn't be as bad as all that, Boy. It'll be too green this time of year to burn much . . . and he never mentioned winds up there."

> *They're burning off at the Rampadelles,*
> *the tawny flames uprise*
> *With greedy licking around the trees;*
> *the fierce breath sears our eyes.*
> *On the runs to the west of the Dingo Scrub*
> *there was drought and ruin and death . . .*

"But, Grandad . . ."
"Get your atlas and let's have a closer look, son."

> . . . *at last one day, at the fierce sunrise,*
> *a boundary rider woke,*
> *And saw in place of the distant haze*
> *a curtain of light blue smoke.*

Monte ransacked his room for his atlas, his imagination in flames, and came back scrummaging through the bruised pages. "That McPherson Range comes a fair way inland, Grandad. See? Look, look!"

"Now calm down," Grandad said, taking the atlas and giving the boy a patting eye. "Look here, the fire's near Canungra on this coastal bulge. Your birds come from up here." A rough finger traced his words. "They're more likely to fly straight down here and over the Denham Range. They're not going to follow the Queensland coast like tourists . . . just to fly over Brisbane. And they don't need refuelling like cars and planes."

"I guess you're right, but . . ."

"No buts about it! You get an early night. Most of those fellas on the wireless don't know much more of what they're talking about than Happee O'Day." Grandad allowed himself a little prejudice to convince the boy.

Nevertheless, Monte kept awake most of the night, afraid if he went to sleep he'd dream of fire engulfing Corker. After all, a bushfire got Bannerman of the Dandenong . . .

> *And in less than a breathing space*
> *Into the gulf of flame was swept*
> *Those laughing eyes and that comely face . . .*

Sounded like a combination of Jerry and Swiftie. He was up before Mrs. Gale's bantams knew it was daylight. Later, Grandad took a pannikin of tea and three thick bricks of toast and jam down to the ducket. They didn't speak. But knew the birds wouldn't be home for long hours yet. The inner beauty of the ugly ducket made it a sanctuary, a refuge with the safety of an ivory tower and the defensibility of a confessional. That morning seemed deracinated from time; the minutes as empty as the first bus to Bora Bora on a Sunday morning, the seconds as full as the last one from Chadla on a Saturday night.

Councillor Duxmann arrived, chauffeured, in the early afternoon with the shiniest unwooden pigeon clock Monte had ever seen. It looked as unreally beautiful as odds and ends he'd noticed in a couple of old movies at a matinee at the Classic Cinema in Kincomba: *Things to Come* and *Just Imagine 1980.*

"What's all this?" Grandad said, greeting the Councillor with the surprise it was.

"To clock in the victor and bring glory to Kincomba and fame to Boomeroo." The man was in full-sail Duxmannese. When Grandad got Monte to come down, he went on: "Listen to it ticking, lad. Like a time bomb ready to blow previous records to Kincomba-come!" That was meant to be the spinnaker going up, but his metaphor was flapping. "The boy's got to get ready for fame and fortune." He tried sidewinding up to Grandad.

"The boy better get ready for a swift kick in the pants if he does too much without my permission," the old man said.

"Teaching him something about real life," Duxmann said.

"All you've taught him so far is something about the other side of his conscience." Grandad wanted to say more, but seeing Monte mesmerized by the new clock recalled flickerings from his own boyhood and suppressed his judgment. Monte had not moved to take the clock, so the old man eased it out of Duxmann's hands and presented it to him. The grandson looked at the grandfather and Duxmann was not there.

"You'll noticed it's sealed," the intruder said. "I've been to Chadla, to the home of your Club's President, and fixed everything." He went on to ask witless questions about pigeons.

Were they edible?

"Like some people make soup from their old boilers when they've finished laying."

"I thought an old boiler was an old moll."

Did they migrate?

"For God's sake, they're homing pigeons!"

Did they ever refuse to fly?

"Birds?"

When several pigeons flew over Boomeroo the Cucumber Councillor bellowed excitedly. "Here they come! Here they are!"

As these birds continued serenely on their way he shook his voice at them until Monte explained they would be the first of the Sydney pigeons.

"There'll be a lot from now on," Grandad said. "Then the best of the Newcastle birds. If the Sydney flocks are coming through Oxford Pass they'll all be flying this way."

"Why don't you go up and sit on the veranda with Grandad?" Monte said, avoiding the look he knew he would get for that suggestion. "My birds ain't used to having anyone round the ducket when they get home."

"Of course, of course. Thoughtless of me," Duxmann allowed. "I'll keep Grandad company."

Grandad grimaced first then winked at Monte, and this generating expression again extinguished the fat man from the shire town. They throttled grins.

Monte lugged his new clock up the ladder, sniggering at the thought of the ear-bashing Grandad was sure to get from the original Mr. Biglips himself. A batch of Newcastle birds finally went over Boomeroo in broad scudding platoons. They flew in fast shafts of conglomerate blue, embroidering themselves in the valley sky.

"No doubt they're only at the Newcastle birds," the Big Boomer said knowingly to Grandad. "Don't excite yourself, old man." The gall of the man came from Calvary — and there were moments when some of his jibes were spears.

"I won't," Grandad said. "I'm too busy figuring out the mileage you're doin' in my rocking chair . . . and why this . . . unimportant thing means anything to you."

The sloppy rocking man was honest for about the third time in his life. "I like to be in everything," he said.

Grandad nodded: there were no words to answer such blatant honesty.

Fifteen minutes after the majority of Newcastle birds had passed over, Monte saw a familiar pair of blue wings topping the schoolyard trees. His heart leapt. It couldn't be Corker. "Corker," he murmured and felt hunch-drunk. She just could not have *not* won. The fastest Newcastle birds would still be almost ten minutes from their duckets.

As the heroine skimmed over Garsides' roof there was a tremendous assembled roar from the kids who had quietly (almost reverently) gathered in Gales' yard. "Yahoo! It's Corker! You bloody beaut!" She had become used to receptions, but had never had one such as this.

Corker slipped into the trap as Monte stooped for the fifteenth time to make sure the smart new clock was alive and ticking. He sprang up joyfully to greet her, but she was already on the floor beside the fountain.

"You little toby," he said. "You know better than that, even if I did forget to put the water lid down."

Alerted by the kids, Duxmann invaded their reunion. "Have you got her, lad?"

"Now you stop that guzzling," Monte said. "Boozing like

Reggie Allsop. You'll be kicking the door down next." He kneeled beside her, his heart and eyes brimming. "See the new clock you won, girl. That silly cow you can hear yelling downstairs finagled it. Hey . . . come here! Come away from that water right this minute."

As he reached for her, his eyes paralyzed his bent arm, stopped the soft spread of his fingers, and arrested his tender presumption.

Corker was leaning against the galvanized iron drinking trough sucking up water . . . and as fast as she did the water and what blood was left in her body wept from her torn breast. She was ripped from breastbone to beak.

"Oh no . . . oh God! Please, no." From the corner of a suffering eye Monte saw her topple into the pool of her own diluted blood.

"Nooooooooooo-ahhhhhhhhhhh!" He electrified the home birds in their compartments and they flew themselves at the wire netting.

"What's the matter up there? Go up and get the clock." Duxmann turned on Grandad.

"Can't do that. And I wouldn't," Grandad said after calling softly to the boy. He was positive Monte would have answered him if there was anything at all he could have done.

"Then I shall." Duxmann grandiose.

Monte picked up Corker and cuddled her to his belly, splashed tears plopping into her blood puddle. "What the hell happened to you?" He tried to nurse her to life.

> *Safe, safe at Namoora gate,*
> *I fell and lay like a stone.*
> *Ah, love, your arms were around me then,*
>   *Your warm tears brought me to life again,*
> *But, oh God . . .*

"Somebody's got to go up there," the Councillor shouted. "Something's wrong!"

"No!" Grandad was firm. "The boy knows I'm here, and that door's rigged. That's the way he's built his life. And nobody's going to break doors down around here, or burst into anybody's life uninvited any more."

Jerry slipped out of the ring of kids who had now surged over Gales' fence and ran through his own yard to his mother, who was drinking beer on the back lawn with Feet-Feet and the Ten-bob Angel.

"I think something's happened to Corker . . . or Monte, and old Duxmann's fit to tear the ducket down." He stood in front of Vonnie Kyle and his eyes examined hers with every skerrick of judgment he could muster. He was afraid of being too old to be crying. He stammered one more word: "Mum?" He shot off to the secret fence trap on his side of the ducket and left Vonnie to her own translation and trepidation.

Feet-Feet bounded up and Vonnie followed, almost knocking over the patio table, which the Angel steadied before going after them. The three whores burst into Grandad's yard like a phalanx of Amazons.

"I'll do it," Duxmann was saying, pushing by Grandad and heading for the ladder.

"Do what?" Vonnie Kyle surged ahead and fronted him. "If there's any tigering going on here, we want to know about it."

The near-raving politician simmered. He hadn't heard Vonnie's tone and thought help had come at last. "Get the ring off that bird up there."

Vonnie was unhesitatingly adamant. "No!" She shook her head. "That's that kid's castle, not your Chambers pisshouse, you gormless fat goat."

"Why you . . ." Duxmann shook off Grandad's provisional hand. "I've used up people like . . ."

"People like who?" Vonnie interrupted. "People like yourself! You're about as much real use to this world as a feather duster."

Feet-Feet heaved her hefty body directly in front of his bellyful of crap. "Keep away from that ladder, you big fat fart." She looked, and was, immovable.

Beautiful and barefooted, Angela glided into position between Vonnie and Feet-Feet. "Your money's run out, honey," she whispered.

The three prostitutes stood their ground like Saints at the Annunciation, without knowing for sure what had happened except that Jerry had pleaded with them ... and Kylie was never the beggar.

"You ain't got enough to pay your way through a penny turnstile for a shit," Duck yelled from the composure of kids, and nobody footed him up the arse or clouted him across the head. The realization amazed him.

"Go home, Duckie," Feet-Feet said, with initiating kindness.

Big Duckie Duxmann looked at her as if he were a rhinoceros contemplating a charge.

"Don't try it," the big moll said and stood straighter, as molded as a Cellini and solid as a brick shithouse, "or I'll go through you like a fine-tooth comb."

Duxmann grrumphed.

"I think you'd better go," Grandad said.

"I do my own thinking," Duxmann snapped, knowing it was no use asking any of that circus of kids to go fetch his chauffeur, who had been told not to leave the car under any circumstances whatsoever.

"Not very well, I'm afraid," Grandad said.

"I've been a good friend," Duxmann said directly to Vonnie.

"If that's a threat," she said, "there's little you can do to or for me now, materially or financially, unless you want to send your wife to see me." The implication was wherever he wanted to find it.

"Ya goin' bad," Duck said, closer and braver.

"Cucumber go home," Li'l Peterdunny piped.
"You kids can all go home now," Grandad said. "Duck
... will you get rid of them for me?"

Duck, who had always dreamed of some given authority, at first looked as though he had been hit by a devil-tailed pitchfork, but when the possibility of glory struck him he shepherded the rubble of children away with an almost Biblical awe.

"Don't cry," Jerry said to Monte, after creeping into the ducket. "Mum-an-the-girls'll fix his cart if old Duxie starts anything."

"Git the hell outa here an' take that flamin' flash clock with you," Monte told him.

Jerry left. He was used to being bawled out by someone he loved. He didn't take the pigeon clock. In the adult world in which the Kyle youngster lived the principle was give and take what you contracted for. Without that fundamental he might never have survived in his brothel home.

After-dark trapped in a few minutes later. She settled on Monte's bossed shoulder and pecked his ear. He knew which bird did that. Temptation revived him: he reckoned he could still clock After-dark in and probably win. His heart was dead but not yet his mind. Although he had not for a second considered taking Corker's ring off the dead body, he did for a moment wonder if he should grab the crown with After-dark. No. How could he pretend to the unclose world that any other bird but Corker had won? Brushing the pecking pigeon from his shoulder he returned to his misery.

"It's all my fault. I killed you. You're just a baby and I killed you." He drew his bones into a bunch and agonized.

Duxmann was now panting and ranting like a pregnant big cat that has something treed, only to find itself surrounded by wild dogs. Vonnie, Feet-Feet and the Angel kept him in their snarly sights. Jerry returned and told them Corker was dead.

"There's nothing at all to keep you in Boomeroo now, Mr. Duxmann," Grandad said. "You should never have come in the first place."

"What a waste of hope," the Councillor said.

"We all feel like a rotten pit prop at times," Grandad consoled him.

"Keep your platitudes to yourself," D.Q. replied, giving the tricky trio an aggrieved look and adding, "What a prize parcel of prostitutes you are!"

"You can also keep your disgusting hypocrisy to yourself," the Ten-bob Angel said.

The big prick from Kincomba gave up: his fat quoit wobbled as he waddled away. He was a sad thing leaving.

Jerry waited in the downstairs ducket after everyone had dispersed, listening to Monte's mourning. Perhaps a tear might drip through the floorboards and anoint his upturned face. He loved, but was (had to be) ashamed of how he loved.

Grandad's love was no mistranslation. He knew the boy would come down some time through the night in his own good unhappy and hopeless time; so he went into the house, had a shot of rum, made a pot of tea, sat at the kitchen table to wait. To be there. This was not another Boadicea incident. This was the night a boy might die and a man be born. This was where the conscience dwelt . . . and that was terminal territory if travelled alone.

13

NEVER AT ANY TIME had Corker come home through Oxford Pass. Ever since her first training flys from Shannondor and Killingworth across the Terribana Hills she had flown through that ridge gap between Kaiser and the first rise of the Terribanas when flying from the north. She later used the higher but shorter route through the contrary Jindaboolawaringoondigi Gap. After that, hugging the eastern slopes of those mountains protected from the south by Mount Kaiser, she would slip through the cleft of the Terribana Hills, home.

The hawks nesting on the rugged mountain fed regularly over the Pass, but on the day of the Coronation Fly, with the Sydney and Newcastle birds closely packed in cavalries of wings, they had little choice of stragglers.

The predators sulked and nagged one another and bitched on smaller birds that weren't worth the eating. Three of them saw the blue-check wings cresting the foothills, cawed convivially, and spread their wings simultaneously . . . and their birdship ended at that.

Any one of them hunting alone could have swooped silently on Corker in midair in a steep stealthy dive, and that would have been that. But their greedy jostling alerted her and, recognizing Bora Bora, she dropped low over the mining townscape as the hawks bothered one another down to follow her across the tops of the coal-dusted houses.

Half a mile from the last roof, as the hunters were preparing a second attack, Corker saw the Boomeroo bus battling along Gutshaker Road and went lower still, hovering above it. The hungry pirates also descended, something else they might never have done alone.

The pigeon was now flying no higher than the telegraph poles, yet the hawks, with a mutually whetted appetite, showed no signs of deserting her. She sought her last refuge in the dusty froth of the gravel road which clung to the rattling bus like a ballooning petticoat. The bus, she knew, like herself, was going home. As she disappeared into the choking wake of the bus the big birds spotted a spring congregation of sparrows rooting the feathers off one another on the long perspective fence that divided the golf links from the pit property, and decided to clip the guts from that randy lot of spugs.

Not knowing this, the blue-checker kept to the haven of the bus dust. Merely a hundred yards before the dry Gutshaker Road bounced into contact with the paved Great North-West Highway one of the bus's rear tires picked up a small jagged bean-can lid and flipped it upwards and backwards. It spun through the churning folds of dust like a sidereal buzz saw, creating new minor galaxies of finer white mist before it stung the pigeon's throat longwise. Corker never knew what happened. She only knew, when the gravel powder dissolved on the highway, she had beaten the hawks home. Her breasts may have felt unusually cold for the warmth of the day and she may have arrived home with an unusually outrageous thirst, but she never really knew what had happened to herself.

And Monte had been waiting. That freckled face. Those

tender fingers. That slightly crow voice. Lighthouse eyes. An unruly rough nest of hair. Boy smell . . .

All that had been worth racing for, above and beyond the fact that flying was life, was waiting in that ducket. It constituted a love for which there was no death. Dying was a realization that enjoined two worlds . . . a shuttle-car process . . . and a wonderful and enduring journey.

Valhalla was.

"Is!" And never again would (or could) Monte be quite so fulfilled or hurt or hyphenated by love.

Beneath the boy-and-his-bird mourning procedure, Jerry waited, eventually inventing one jealous halcyon tear, as semiprecious as olivine, to remain greener than boyhood. In time boyhood became a varicolored cargo of memory . . . a stolen tapestry of hope shot in roses and reality; the beginning to the acceptance of a life he would be afraid to be proud of. For all that it might be a forthright life, inviolable it could never be. To live is to love, to love whatever the mind dictates to the heart.

Jerry retreated quietly, went home and locked himself in his bedroom — where the whores left him alone because they imagined he, too, would be heartbroken like Monte — where he masturbated with a photograph of Montgomery Clift Monte had given him. Kissing the gentle, promising paper mouth, his heart argued against the loss of what his body never really wanted.

Nursing Corker to the grave, Monte was sure he would never feel pain or love again; was positive that he would die of grief. Firmly believing his body would remain as dead as his heart and brain, he put the light little corpse in a shoe box, covering it with pigeon peas before he lidded it, and buried it in no-man's-land, stomping the earth down so that no one except himself would ever know where Corker lay.

"But you'll hear me, little fella: every time I go to the

pigeon ducket and walk over your grave, you'll hear me. And you'll be able to hear me whistlin' the birds in. And nobody else — not even Grandad — will know where you are. Except . . . maybe . . . some day, if I have a little boy and he wants to fly pigeons . . . maybe I'll tell him where you are. Oh . . . oh, God, how can you be so fuckin' cruel? She was such a little thing."

Going into the house, where he knew Grandad would be waiting, Monte was convinced that he would never feel horny again. *Don't matter: I never did like the smell of spoof.*

"You didn't have to wait up, Grandad; but I knew you would."

"That's why I did."

"Gee, Grandad . . . there ain't much to anything. I don't feel like . . . goin' on."

"You will."

"Why?"

Grandad drew him in and enfolded him. "Because I'm a selfish *old man* and I need you. I love you, Boy. Your life is so much my life. Keep living it for me."

"Oh . . . Grandad."

"Cry if you want to, Richard. Don't be an emotional dwarf like a lot of men. There's a helluva lot of love in tears. It's all right, son. Let it out."

Cry he did. After the deluge, Grandad suggested that he should go to bed and sleep another day of his life away. "You can afford it."

"If I do, you reckon my birthday might come a day sooner?"

"You wouldn't have something in mind?"

"Maybe."

"Like a new pigeon basket?"

"Exactly!" Monte spun backwards before he left the kitchen. "You know," he said, "you're a good old man . . .

a bugger of a grandfather but a good old man." He laughed a little deliriously before he promised: "I te'ya what . . . I'll never bloodywell cry again. I feel like I'm waterlogged after swimmin' in the creek all day."

"We won't cavil about that now."

"I want to cavil!"

"You are a little bastard at times. Let's say that . . . just as a white leghorn has so many eggs in her, healthy people have so many tears in them. And you *are* healthy."

The kid waved his hand down jestingly and demanded: "Wake me when the sugar's melted on me porridge."

14

MONTE RENEGED ON SCHOOL for the rest of the week and Grandad allowed him this time for grief. By Saturday the noises of the town began to penetrate his misery and he said to himself, "Boy, you can't sit here on your coign for a donkey's age. You gotta do something."

Going out into the back yard, he spread his feet, raised his arms and stretched his fattening neck while a gentle rain played on his nose-high face. A sunshower. What a lovely word! He looked towards the Dividing Range. Suddenly . . . Ol' Man Kaiser copped him through the drizzle like a visible echo of something Grandad had said. His pushbike came out of the washhouse faster than a disturbed wasp from a half-made clay nest.

Not fully knowing what he wanted to do, he pedalled out of town in a precious frenzy. A mile or so along Gutshaker Road he took the old steepening twin-rutted dray track to Stinking Biddy Springs at the knees of Mount Kaiser. Biking up the long drive to the Springs, he wondered if he ought to drown himself. "Bet I'd stink more than old Biddy did," he said to a bright rush of reddies fluttering from wattle tree to bottlebrush. "Then the kids'd call it Stinking Howdie Springs."

The sun came out to permit the bush its celebration. He saw birds as pretty as porcelain salt and pepper shakers bracing themselves dry in fits and starts. A long skinny lizard as defiant as a tree landlord snapped a tongue at him. A cow as motherly as Mrs. Gale flicked her tail. From nowhere a deliriously happy dog charged a bevy of scrub quail almost through his wheels. Rabbits as quizzical as Easter Bunnies alerted their ears to the creak of the bike chain, then stiffened like statues. An old horse questioned his straining movements as he lifted his arse from the leather leaf-shaped seat and pressed each pedal with frantic weight.

At first he intended to leave his bike at Black Douggie's humpy, but there was a bike already there suspiciously like Swiftie's; so he left his own in a bottleneck of bracken. He didn't even want Swiftie to know what he was doing (whatever he was doing) in this elbow of the woods. None of the half-caste kids punching around the huts saw him.

The track looped and lost itself among a picnic of fish fern in the middle of an elite hatch of bee-festooned wattle trees — those bees were so honey happy they didn't mind his wading through. Their pollen-crazy hum forecast a warm and early summer. He trudged on, winding his watch: it was eleven.

Monte heard a scurried whisper, cocked his ears and held his breath. "Ah, you're hearing things." It was Swiftie's voice. He opened his mouth to call, but for some shifty reason breathed in cautiously instead and sneaked forward. Not ten feet away, beyond a gallant tree fern, Swiftie Madison was pumping his body on top of a young girl's. Fucking the life out of himself and into her. Literally rootin' Christ out of her. Terry? Fascinated, he watched his mate's desperate movements. He was good at it. Swiftie *could* fuck.

The girl's knees were up each side of Swiftie's backside, as though she was keeping him on a track, because he sure as hell was puffing like a stream train. His light tan body shining against her ash-grey skin; his white arse like two neat round balloons.

She was whimpering. "Oh-Swiftie-Swiftie. It feels so nice with you. Lovely-loveleee! Keep doin' it to me."

It was Miriam Trader pressed beneath Swiftie. She was one of the young gins from Stinking Biddy: her big bugged-out ears betrayed her even though he could not see a lot of her face. Buglugs Trader?

"Bejesus!" Swiftie cried, in that way Monte had heard him express excitement a thousand times, as he plunged like a gull after a fish. "Holy-Jesus-fuckin'-Christ! I'm comin'! I'm shootin' me bolt! I'm gonna fill ya twat with spoof." There was a renewed bucking of bodies, then the sudden death of all movement. Swiftie sighed: "And Jesus said, I have come."

"I liked it," Miriam murmured. "Did you like it?"

"It was bloody beaut," Swiftie said. "I'm gonna fuck the arse off you all summer, Buglugs."

"And will I be your girl?"

"Sure." Swiftie could be more surely automatic when it came to lying than any other boy in town.

"And will you call me Miriam insteada Buglugs?"

"When we're by ourselves if you want." Swiftie eased himself up. "Whew!" He patted his prick with pride — it was still stiff and inquisitive — then looked around questioningly before he hollered: "Didya get a good look, Duck?"

"What's the matter?" Miriam hunched her body into a question mark.

"I got a feelin' someone's out there watchin' us," Swiftie said. "Probably Duck Allsop. He's the greatest rock-spider in Australia." He cupped a tunnel of fingers to his mouth and shouted. "Hang around and watch some more, Ducksa! I'm gonna fuck 'er again. Then I'm comin' out there to find you and beat all hell-shit outa ya, you poofter spy."

Boggle-eyed, Monte backed away in silent awe. Swiftie's prick sure had grown through the winter. It was now bigger than Grandad's when he got out of a warm tub. Yet last summer, swimming in the creek in the nuddy, Swiftie's dick had been barely half an inch longer than his own. Monte felt himself: it was as hard as a bike handle, but only about half as big as the rubber handle-grip. Swiftie's prick had to be about five inches . . . and still hard.

He instinctively sidled away, uncalled-for tears in his eyes. It would never be the same. Swiftie had stolen boyhood from all the gang. They would never be kids again. Boys but not kids. Little crippled memories fell around him. Maybe Swiftie had been right after all when he said, "Ya gotta keep it growin'! You've gotta whock-ya-cock at least twice a night to remind it what it's for."

"Let's have another go," he heard Swiftie say and couldn't resist another look back. He saw Maddo kick Miriam's legs apart as though they were bark before he dropped on top of her again. It hurt him to see how uncaring his mate could be.

Maybe once you had a real fuck you'd never want to play with yourself again . . . or with a mate. Wonder if you had a mother and she caught you at it . . . what'd she do about it? Plodding on in mind and body, Monte figured it would be fun to have a mother. She'd have hot johnnie cakes waiting for you after school in winter. With warm treacle. Like Gloamy's mother did. Someone to smoodge up to like Batter's Mum, who often gave him an extra zac without telling his old man. Even Vonnie Kyle sometimes gave Jerry thin bread and butter with cocoa on a cold night. And Mrs. Madison was a real sport. She acted the nanny with Swiftie. They'd singalong together when there was a popular song on the wireless:

*We're Up From Down Under,
From Down Under where
A spinner is a cove whose pennies . . .
Git in the copper's hair.
Up From Down Under,
From Down Under the moon
Where a cockatoo is a bloke who sits . . .
In fronta the billiard room.*

"Go, Mum, go!" And Swiftie would jig around her. Of course, she'd bat him over the head if she heard him singing the dirty version:

*Where a bastard is a sonofabitch
But only if he's a friend.*

Wonder what she'd say if Swiftie went home today and said: "Hallo, Mum. It's *me* your *favorite and only son*, Terreeeee. Guess what I've been up to all arvo, Mum? I've been up Buglugs Trader . . . that's who I've been up all arvo, Mummo!" Monte giggled to himself.

Soon he began to scramble up towards the Redbutts, the shoulders of the mountain. The monkey vines caught at his throat and wild raspberry bushes tripped him. Spring was choking the bush with delight. It would have been easier going in the summer after the kids and their fellow-enemies had range-warred through. When lovers, smitten by September, had roamed deep to find hidden fucking spots, crushing the maidenhair fern beneath their striving bodies, deflowering the young wattle and gum shoots. After that greatest Peeper since Tom, Duck Prick-puller Allsop, had made watching bowers where he could lie in comfort and see the sex-active grubs and molls at it, beat his own meat and pleasure himself with some smooth thick stick.

Even if Duck had copped Swiftie at Buglugs and spread the word, Swiftie wouldn't give a rat's shit. He'd just say,

"Listen, Duckfuck, I don't care if you tell the bloody world . . . I've read the comic book. I'm a . . . adulterator, and I got a stinkin' big scarlet *A* on me dong." Then he would laugh that great walloping laugh of his. Oh, Swiftie!

"Terry Madison," Miss Cruikshank had said. "I checked the library cards and you haven't taken either one of the two suggested novels out for this year. Neither *A Tale of Two Cities* nor *Les Misérables*."

"But I read both the comic books, Miss Cruikshank . . . and I studied and compared them. I know all about Sydney Carton, Jean Valjean and Fantette and . . ."

"Then from the store of your comic-book knowledge perhaps you'd tell us your favorite character from one of these books . . . and why?"

Swiftie may have been a Tartar in many ways but he was no dumb bunny. He stood up, went straight to the blackboard and printed: "Eponine." "She knew what she wanted and went about it," he said facilely.

Cruikshank tried unsuccessfully to stifle a smile: her Prince had done it again.

But . . . shit . . . the fuss the blokes made around the billiard room about girls was . . . Shit . . . what was so marvelous about twat?

"Give it to me seven times a week an' I'll never die hungry," Gutsa Mevinney said.

"Your moll would choke to death, but." Everybody knew Gutsa had a strange-shaped prick like a pear, as though his balls had been molded to the shaft.

In billiard-roomese and bar-speak, women were molls and anybody who wasn't a mate was a grub. Grubs and molls seemed to populate the country.

But there had to be more to it than what hit the eye. If it had satisfied Swiftie so much why did he have to go back to it right away? Monte always felt a bit exhausted and regretful after whacking off.

"It makes you think, Essie," Mrs. Allsop said, "how

lucky we women are . . . being the wanted ones, I mean. If it was the other way round I couldn't be bothered racin' round everywhere looking for it with my tongue hanging out like the men do."

Coming to a fortress of lantana, Monte had to backtrack until he found a way between some lillipilli trees he never knew existed. What did it matter now? The Lillipilli Raiders will never ride again. By the time he burst into unfiltered sunlight beneath a rock shoulder it was after midday. He piddled in several nice circles then in two smaller dribbly ones. The pattern looked like a good secret sign for some society. Like the one always advertised in the Sunday papers promising the Secret Of Life.

"What's this secret of life all about, Grandad?"

"There isn't any secret to life, Boy."

"Well, what do you mean?"

"God knows! But I can tell you one of the nearest things to such a secret that I've discovered about life . . . in two words."

"In just two bloody words?"

"I didn't say *that*."

"In two words, well."

"Keep busy."

"Is that all? I sorta expected something . . . fabulous."

"Everybody expects too much. You have to fulfill your own life, Boy. No matter if you're big or little, young or old, you've got to keep your mind and body busy or you . . . just go to seed."

Moving away from his urine artistry, Monte spreadeagled himself on a warm flat ledge of stone and let the sun stake him. Lying on his back, it seemed that Mount Kaiser surpassed the sky. He closed one eye and the mountain leant over him; it looked like the most enormous thing in the world.

"What is the biggest thing in the world?"

"Young Henry Garside's whangeroo!"

"What *is* the biggest thing in the world, Miss Cruikshank?" Tiny David Petersen wanted to be afforded peace.
"Man's mind."
"But what would be the greatest thing to do?" Sarah Connelly from nowhere Neave's Gully asked.
"To live. To meet life and be alive. Sometimes it's noisy and apparent, sometimes silent and waiting. It's all life. Living *is*."

Jumping up upon that recollection Monte decided to climb to the big wind-chiselled cave called Kaiser's Ear. Hustling wildly at first, childlike in desperation, he grabbed anything within reach until a warped scrubby shrub gave way holus-bolus and left him teetering. Shivering, he pressed his body into the mountainside. When he was game enough to look down he saw the weedy traitor bush caught on the horn of a crevice and his balls shrivelled. "Hell . . . me balls have shrunk into me guts."

After that he snuggled his way up to the lobed sandbed of the cave and was relieved to find it firm and molded by the winter rain. Gaining his angle of balance, he walked up, surfie-like, feeling akin to an Aboriginal god. "If I was an Abo god I bet Miriam Trader would give me more twat than Swiftie."

Sitting in the cave listening to the wind make rhinal noises as it swiped Kaiser's face, he looked down across the valley and wondered where his heart was. The Stinking Biddy Springs track threaded its way through the bush like two strands of fawn cotton. Wonder why old people say threadle a needle? And why Tony Delarue calls a reel of cotton, thread?

Gutshaker Road gashed the valley between Bora Bora and Boomeroo. Dooragul Creek looked like a huge snake on a snakes-and-ladders board. The railway line might have been Jerry's Hornby train set. The new Chadla racetrack was definitely Swiftie's Totopoly. "He won't be spending much more time playing that. Too busy running his legs off looking for sheilas. Shit! I wish I was Peterdan's age again." The sound of his own voice wasn't exceptionally comforting.

It was well after one o'clock. "I'll keep that friggin' new pigeon clock. Ain't giving up flying my pigeons. Not for a dozen Buglugs. And I'm sure as hell not givin' that clock back to that Councillor coot."

There was a ridge above the ear-cave which gave access to an oblique ravine that ran almost to the top of the mountain. He decided it was worth trying to reach the back of Kaiser's Head . . . now that he was halfway there.

From this sand base a narrow ledge led out to the carved rock cheek. He moved cautiously, like a fly reading braille, surprised to find the Aboriginal carvings which seemed so interesting from below meant next to nothing close up. Body close to the mountain, he edged out and slowly up. This ledge narrowed from about a foot to a few inches near the nose; but there, nearly four feet above, was another ledge that seemed wider, although it, too, narrowed as it climbed back above the cave once more and led to another higher ledge. This pattern was repeated and the kid knew from postcards he and Swiftie had snitched from the paper shop that these five galleries were much of a muchness in their . . . ancient intagliated symmetry.

Cruikshank loved that one. "Intagliated." She savored the word. "Carved in depth. Sunken in design, not carved in relief. Your Grandmother's cameo would *not* be a good example, Bettina, so put your hand down? 'Intagliate' . . . to cut a design in a flat surface. And don't get too ambitious, Boy Howard. Remember the child who learnt that wild meant frantic and then went into the bush to pick some frantic flowers?"

Shuffling and hugging his way, Monte came to the last foot of the first ledge. He reached up and got a finger-grip on the one above. It was lipped and firm. Pretending he was pulling himself out of the Tuggeroo Baths without the buoyancy of the water beneath him, he muttered. "To hell with Archimedes' Principle . . . God, gimme a hand!"

As he pulled himself painstakingly up, his eyes crawled along the higher ridge and his toes sucked into the wall face. "Christ, how do flies do it?"

On the gallery wall above, about a foot from his nose, there was a crack and he crept his fingers towards it without relieving them of the burden of his body. This unholy effort left a corresponding weakness in his other hand and he felt those fingers unboning themselves. A giant gap of time threatened him. He grabbed quickly and grabbed surely, and jammed his knuckles into the crack until they bled, then began to ride one knee up the rock surface until he had his right leg lying along the upper ledge. In this comparatively safe position he rested, thinking about a Tom and Jerry cartoon without knowing he was reviewing plausible impossibilities. "Talk about being shit-scared." Neither Tom nor Jerry answered him.

Sweating and shivering, he pulled the rest of himself up and got to his feet again. He was now out beyond the shoulder of the mountain and there were hundreds of feet of cliff face between him and the belly of the bush. The biggest and highest of the gum trees would share bits and pieces of his body if he fell from here.

"An' they'll scrape the rest of me up in Mt. Isa. 'Member the day you threw a razor blade into Stinking Biddy Springs . . . into the clear smelly-deep water . . . and watched it drift and glide to the bottom . . . glinting like imprisoned sunlight sending messages into space. Well . . . if you fall now, Boy, you won't drift and glide like that razor blade. You'll bloodywell fall, whap-bang, like a stupid bird that forgot its wings. Splut!"

Pressing his face to the primitive rock-cheek, he wondered if from the valley he looked like one of the carvings. He was nearly pissing himself with fear as he moved upward towards the third shelf. But I just had a bigger piddle than a pet pony. He believed that being afraid was OK with God. Still, he knew perfectly well at that moment there was more fear in his heart than there was God.

When he reached up for the next ledge he knew he was beaten. It was not lipped but marble-smooth and it sloped down. It would be easier to try to get a hold on the dome of the Kincomba Council Chambers. The cutting of the native legend wasn't deep enough to give him a worthwhile foothold. At this point, the sandy fan-shaped lobe of the cave was more than thirty feet below. Suddenly the climbing wasn't important. Grandad and the pigeons and the old house mattered most.

By the time he realized this thought his fingers were giving way in conjecture with messages decoded too soon from his subconscious and he hadn't the pinch of a chance to regain his balance. As he began to fall the same belly-terror that assailed him at Christmas and Easter when he walked into church with Grandad knotted his bravery.

"You think God knows what we're up to most of the time, Grandad?"

"You mean does he keep score?"

"Yes."

"I doubt it. The way these do-gooders go on," Grandad said, "God must be kept so bloody busy telling them what not to do — there are millions of goody-goodies in touch with him constantly — he doesn't have time to check up on the sinners."

"Well, why do we come twice a year?"

"You come because I bring you and I come because Granma used to take me with her at Christmas and Easter. It's not much to do for her memory."

"It don't hardly seem enough, Grandad," Monte said, clenching his stomach with a sentimental power that frightened him.

"Nobody ever does enough for others. Not even for those they love the most, Boy. Men are like that. Don't seem to have that little extra needed to fill themselves . . . before they can help fill others. Don't worry about it. You're doing fine in your own way and time. You're going to be a good man some day."

Monte ground his teeth to stop from hollering on the way down. A tremendous shining dawn enveloped him as one of his knees cracked against the eave of the cave. He never remembered being trampolined by the sandbed. He came back to daylight when his hip hit the first rocks, which bounced him into a clutching colony of scrub gums. He did have time to think: I'm not doing so bloody fine right now.

Octopus roots, sharp grass, biting weeds and grinding gravel patches all had a go at him. They were emery cruel to his skin. Like a clacking lottery wheel his body spun down the blurred mountainside, now a rough blanket folding over him, now a jigsaw of nature fermenting beneath him. Fountains of stars spilled out of his head. One last kind bush nursed him for an instant above the spot where he'd piddled. He saw pissy circles within the hazy shades of spring billowing around him, like urinal solar systems before his eyes, whirling faster and boring closer. A dizzy universe, keeping itself very bloody busy indeed . . . Grandad would like that. He felt fey and brave now; cleaner than heaven but dirtier than the Devil; dumber than Duck and wiser than Miss Cruikshank; more poised than Goldie Killorn; as slovenly as Buglugs Trader . . . Giddier than a Catherine wheel on cracker night.

His watch hit him in the eye and in a mid-mental chiaroscuro he thought: "I'll still have it with me the day I die, Miss Killorn. Crikey! But not yet?"

A last surf of pain broke over his carcass as loud taratantaras burst his eardrums and a fantastic freckling of stars, moons and asterisks rose and fell and set in his tired irises. A soundless blackness lifted him above the motile flowermouth of a feathered waterspout, and the swirling commotion turned to probing plumes . . . blue and white and bleeding. Strange concentric little shutter-eyes blinking at him. Then the melting into tears. And then peace.

"Sometimes it's noisy and apparent, sometimes silent and waiting."

"To live!" Oh, Miss Cruikshank, I'm too young to die. Save me with your all-knowingness.

Life is like a gather of molten glass: death is the same gob at the moment the glassblower ceases to breathe shape into it. Its creation is complete. Same gob of glass: some difference.

"You can stuff all that bullshit up your glory-hole, mate!"

"Death is a threshold."

"Life's fuckin' better."

"It sure as hell beats death."

All I wanted was to live long enough to be old enough to go on the piss with the Boomeroo Bulls . . . that's all.

"Come on, Rita. Quit worrying about the future. Turn you cardy right side out an' we'll go along to Esmeralda and get our teacups read. You can't get a better two-and-sixpenny future this side of the undertaker's."

I don't want to die now because I haven't figured out whether I'll go to heaven or Valhalla. If you give me a choice, God, I wanna be with Corker.

Life *is* better, but!

"Keep breathin'."

To live. Living *is*.

"Gi'-us a fair go at it, God."

Death is for moths on a Friday night and frogs that try to cross the highway; goldfish that jump too high and flies that get into the kitchen when Sunday dinner's being served; Aldertons' chooks and Catholic saints.

"The fact that there are no living saints should not be solace for sinners," Father Barry preached.

"Wonder how I get in touch with Buddha?"

15

IT WAS ALMOST AN HOUR before Monte came to. His watch was in his eye and when he lifted his head an excruciating guillotine dropped on the back of his neck. "Now I know how Sydney Carton felt. It's three o'clock and I'm not dead . . . and my watch is goin' bloody better than I am."

One forearm was lying beneath Monte's face and, looming large under the buttress of his upper arm, an ant moved through the undergrass into his clearing vision. "Where's the rest of the wagon train, ant? I thought you guys moved in Big Trails like John Wayne." The ant seemed inconvenienced and changed direction. "You won't find much round here 'cept us dinosaurs." The ant (he imagined) looked as perplexed as Gutsa Mevinney had.

"Where you two kids goin'?" Gutsa grabbed Monte by the collar and blocked Swiftie's path with hooves bigger than a blacksmith's sign. Talk about prehistoric monsters.

"Up the hill to skin a dinosaur," Swiftie said, grimacing with his broadening hands.

"Balls," Gutsa said. "Them things live in Russia. I saw pictures in the barber-shop magazine."

"You're talking about a Russian mammoth," Monte said. "This is just a prehistoric pile of bones at Biddy. Probably some Dreamtime kangaroo . . . you know?"

"Say!" Gutsa said. "Maybe that's what made that place stink . . . in the first place. Hell, I never did believe all that shit about old Stinkin' Biddy."

He let them pass, his face a cartoon of incipient wonder.

Monte pushed himself over onto his back. It hurt like hell. Maybe all the worthwhile things *are* out there somewhere else in the world, but they sure ain't here. "We got ants and bloody bushflies."

Out there . . . in the beautifully worded West: Dakota, Colorado, Montana, Nevada . . .

"I know *Nevada* is your favorite Zane Grey, Grandad, but I like *The Spirit of the Border* best."

. . . Rio Grande, Red River, Laredo and . . . Cheyenne. Always Cheyenne. It came to him often, like a lullaby someone may have crooned to him before he was old enough to remember faces rather than voices. Some people went to England. Some to Switzerland. New York. The Catholics went to Rome. But Cheyenne was waiting for Boy Howard and he didn't know why. The confession always came with a bloopy eye.

One eye was tear-blooped right now. He had shut the other eye because it was less painful closed. His nose ached and when he managed to feel it it was soft and bloody. "Broken again!"

"You'll end up with a nose like Louis Wolheim," Grandad said after the cricket fiasco.

His arms and legs were scratched, gashed, stiff with pain and stiffer with dried blood. The sun operated on him. Then the flies found him and his thirst began to frighten him. He couldn't move his right leg. The sun continued to give him its undivided attention, encouraging him to doze off, but the thought of food and water grabbed him. "I better git back to Boomeroo before I worry about where the world is."

"Nobody cares about Korea," Tony Delarue said one Sunday in Canwell's Motor Showroom.

"Because the world is too well off," Mr. Canwell said.

"The world is getting too fat to help itself," Cornell Leslie said, purring over a new Sunbeam.

Monte left them agreeing with one another in their adult conspectus. It was easy for them to talk. They'd been places. To war. Come from America. To England. Cornell Leslie had even been to Nairobi . . . Tarzan territory. They had proved for their own satisfaction that the world was there. But where the hell where? How far away in boy-time and -distance?

Clouds began throwing blotted shadows. He screwed himself round and figured he could hop or crawl or drag himself to Stinking Biddy Springs by dark. He knew Black Douggie would always take him in to town in his sidecar: it was Saturday, after all. "I reckon if he can cart his Mum [Big Fat Nellie] round in that contraption I'd be able to lie flat-out in it. Holy mackerel, I'm dyin'f thirst."

He tried pushing his body up onto the stalk of the good leg, but the gammy one folded beneath the initial effort and he collapsed in a pile of agony. His atavistic mind pricked him. Hell, those early convicts took two hundred lashes for breakfast. Five hundred and they went back to work. It took two thousand lashes — prescribed and rationed out by a doctor — to kill them.

Scrabbling for a branch, he forced himself up and leant on his makeshift crutch. Through a gutter in the trees he could see a patch of the lake. There was a V-J rollicking along towards the Tuggeroo Sailing Club jetty, its spark-

white spinnaker looking like a welding flash on the metallic sheen of water. "That'll be Troopa Garrison or Knickers Johnson. They can sail the canvas off the other kids."

There was a kite puttering in the sky. Connie Delarue for sure. She was kite-happy and uncanny with them. It was like a stitch in the sky. Connie could tell you at a glance what was the matter with your kite. Too wide, too short . . . tail too lumpy . . . frame not strong enough for how big you'd made it. "If she was a bit older I'd cottononter 'er and make Swiftie jealous." But Connie would make a better mate than girlfriend. The kite itself was becoming laced with sunthrown dye.

He breathed a mighty John Wayne sigh and turned to Red River Kid Clift, now beside him:

There may be a chance for one;
I'll stop and fight with the pistol here.
You take to your heels and run . . .

Dunn may have left Gilbert, but Kid Clift leave Boy Howard? You gotta be out of your masturbating mind. On a Saturday arvo . . . about the time the matinee was ending in Boomeroo? Leave Boy Howard with a buggered-up leg, a gluey eye, a sun-stitched, rebroken six-stitcher nose, a ripped hip and a God-knows-what kind of guillotine neck? Montgomery Matthew Garth Clift leave him to the embrace of the bushflies and Indian ants? Piss off! You gotta be living in some other anti-infra-Red-River world to even think about it.

"You'd 'aveta be crook, mate."

After hopping a few yards Monte lost his balance and began to elbow-crawl his way along . . . the way the Marines did it in the Hollywood war.

"Keep ya butt down!" The Sergeant bawled from some cinema distance. "Or you'll lose more than ya pants pocket."

Three-striped drongo . . . fancy tryin' to tell Errol how

to win a war? Like tryin' to teach Duck's mother to talk or Ben Leslie to screw.

"John Wayne's better than Errol," Batter said.

"Well . . . Errol's more of a shaggin' man," Swiftie said. He was Flynn-struck and once they called him Ol' Flynn-fucker Madison . . . long before any of them had ever milked their first spoof from long-beaten cocks.

"I read where this Director, John Ford, tells Wayne what to do. Errol's on his own."

"Not in bed he ain't," Gloamy said.

I wish I had John Ford here right now to tell *me* what to do.

"What do I have to remember most?" The adoring rookie questioned John Wayne.

"Don't die!" Big John said.

"Wonder if Montgomery Clift will ever make another cowboy picture?"

"Don't matter . . . they'll never be another Matthew Garth."

"I was glad when that sheila copped the arrow in 'er tits, but."

"Yeah!"

"Those guitar cowboys give me the shits."

"Yeah!"

"When they sing they look like Duck's dirty big black retriever tryin' to shit after it swallowed those billiard balls we smothered with Vegemite."

Monte came to a naked plate of rock. His throat was as dry as a shed snakeskin. Straining his whole body, he looked round and up at Mount Kaiser. "I ain't dead yet, ya big prick! An' I'll be back with ropes an' picks an' all that Hillary gear. And I'm gonna climb farther up you than Swiftie ever got up Buglugs today. You'll keep! You can't get any bigger, but I can. And I got the time . . . 'cause the world ain't gonna end tomorrow."

Caked with pulpy dirt, knitted skin and blood, his knees stinging like billio — he'd ripped his handkerchief cornerways and tied half around each kneecap — he raised one hand and pointed it forward in a manner to make John Ford's Seventh Cavalry proud, and shouted, "Hoh!"

He was not alone. Vague ecstatic shapes mustered around him. Delirious he may have been, but they were more than phantoms. So, Richard-Montgomery-Clift-Gilbert-Hall-Wayne-Flynn-Howard dragged himself down from the jungles of Burma, out of Texas and across the Badlands of Dakota, through Van Diemen's Land and over the Weddin' Mountains to Abilene, with Ben Hall holding off the troopers and their narks, John Wayne and Errol Flynn slaughtering Japs faster than they could yell *Sukiyaki*, Johnnie Gilbert riding point and keeping an eye out for Black Douggie's humpy, and Matthew Garth Clift keeping the whole bloody Apache nation at bay behind him — without getting his pants pocket shot off, and nary an arrow up his arse.

"Don't die!" You can bet your Red River remuda on that.

"I wouldn't mind betting the world's never going to end, Grandad."

"God's too smart for that," Grandad said. "He wouldn't want us all at the same time, like at a Judgment Day corroboree. That wouldn't teach anybody anything. I think God thinks if He teaches us a few at a time the rest will get the lesson eventually. Then again, Boy . . . sometimes I think we're all a little bit of God and it takes the whole shebang to make One God."

Monte massaged his bleeding elbows. "Bloody God sure gave me a good lesson today."

The shadows he crawled through were now getting colder: the sunlight when it flushed him was less comforting. Keep goin', Boy, Monte Ol' Prick! You ain't often wrong but you're right again. You'll make it by dark. As long as you don't run into a trapdoor spider. Hey, Matthew, ride up and tell Gilbert we're takin' a breather soon . . . and how far's the Big Stinky? And while you're there, Bejesus, get rid of that drongo I can hear playin' a guitar and singin' fuckin' "Wagon Wheels" . . . oh, and ain't it about time you took that bleedin' arrow out'f that poor sheila's tits and stuck somethin' else into 'er? I'd rather watch Montgomery Clift fucking that sort than see Swiftie screwin' Buglugs Trader. I'll give *him:* And-Jesus-said-I-have-come. Wonder how far that ant got? Must be awful to be an ant and not have an inkling how big and wide the world. At least I got a-inkling . . . and that's about all I've got . . . an' a bloody little inkling at that. It's a heaped-up bloody world that's what it bloody is!

I could drink a gallon of lolly-water without pissing. I bet Kincomba's just a piddle in the ocean and fatty Duxmann's not even a big drip. I bet there's more world out there than the whole town can imagine.

Monte felt crushed by the world's vastness: lands as inescapable as continents of time, oceans with the scent of centuries behind them, men bigger and hungrier than boyhood ignorance could endure.

Oh Grandad, I need you!

By the time he was within earshot of Stinking Biddy Springs and heard the shouting and screaming of the half-caste kids — who had found his bike and were riding the rusty guts out of it, in and around the lamplit shanties — he was half dead but so embosomed in his delirious imaginings he didn't care.

A pair of small ash-brown feet were planted in front of him. He looked up and saw a pair of terrified baby eyes, framed in a little black face of wonder, goggling down at him. The skinny trunk of a boy, petrified for the recognizing moment. Then the apparition disappeared with a yell. "It's him . . . 'e's ova'ere!"

With his last muscle of will power Monte rolled over

on his back: he heard racing steps and then Swiftie's blessed voice. "Holy Moses, Howdie! Where the fuck you been?"

"I'm buggered, mate."

Swiftie knelt in the dirt beside him and nursed his head. "The kids found your bike hours ago. It scared the livin' daylights out of me when you didn't come back before dark." He turned to the biggest kid in the gathering. "Nutsa . . . rip back and get a water bag. And get Black Douggie!"

"Swiftie . . . I . . ."

"Shut up . . . you silly bastard." Terry patted Monte's cheek and made him more comfortable between his knees. "I got a surprise for you, Monteroo . . . I been fuckin' Buglugs Trader all arvo, and I got her young sister . . . the one they call the Poddy Calf . . . all lined up for you this summer."

"I don't need any of your old ring-ins! I'll get me own roots." Monte smiled to himself in the enshadowed darkness.

"Rest your gob," Swiftie said. "And your dick. It's gonna get a lot'f wear soon."

Monte crept his fingers through the dirt till they found Swiftie's ankle and he squeezed it for lack of adequate breath.

"You and me will probably be the youngest kids in Boomeroo ever to get the pox. That beats divin' off the Highway Bridge, don't it?"

His head now resting on Swiftie's fat prick and soft balls, Monte sighed. His eyes were getting used to the deep sapphire veil of the bush darkness. Swiftie, grinning down at him, winked. A lifetime of friendship in the tick of an eye.

Maybe there were things as good as boyhood in the future. Maybe even better? "Oh fuck, Swiftie," he said, heart-brokenly unsure.

" 'Member the day you asked Cruikshank about 'fuck.' " Swiftie caressed his forehead and pushed back a few over-riding spines of cluttered hair.

"The word 'fuck,' Miss Cruikshank?"

Miss Cruikshank met the request with her normal invincible gaze. " 'Fuck' is both a verb and a noun. A very basic word . . . denoting that ultimate beauty which two people may aspire to . . . and achieve . . . by . . . linking their bodies in love. Later in your lives, you may expand this understanding as your own bodies and the demands of your emotions grow. And your minds will decide for you whether this glorious exercise is merely an amoral pastime or the celebration of a bond in marriage and its purpose of creation. I myself was never one for thinking that a thing or action or person had to be approved of by the police to be holy. However . . . Master Howard, I shall have to give you two hundred lines: ' "Fuck" is not a word normally used in polite mixed company.' Perhaps by the time you have written this down two hundred times the word will have lost some of its billiard-room meaning for you."

"Thank you, Miss Cruikshank."

For everything!

"It's gettin' cold, Swiftie."

"Black Douggie will be here, don't worry. We'll get you back to your place. Don't die, Nelson."

"Kiss me, Hardy?"

Swiftie kidded with his crotch. "Shit, it's nowhere near hard . . . soft as a cabbage fart. Next time it's hard I'll get the Poddy Calf to kiss it for you. Here's the water now!"

"Terry?"

"What? Sip it slowly."

"Was it really that good? I saw you with Miriam Trader."

"Bejesus, I *knew* there was someone out there," Swiftie said. "It was all right. Like sorta as if your heart was spinning in your head. Like as if this great feelin' in your prick was worth dyin' for." Swiftie propped him up while he drank, then eased him back to his groin pillow.

"You weren't very nice to her . . . afterwards," Monte said.

"I gave her ten bob!"

"Jerry said you've been flush. You win the lottery?"

"You wouldn't wanta know."

"Why?"

"I been goin' up to Old Rowlandson's two nights a week. He sucks me off. Gives me a quid."

"Oh, shit! You *can* trust me, but."

"I know that, y'idiot. I missed you more than ever this winter, mate. You always seem to have so much to do in the pigeon season."

"We're gonna stick together from now on," Monte said.

"Like the stamp said to the envelope," Swiftie said. They rested, waiting for Black Douggie and his gondola, creating a memory that would never be exorcized: something to become a part of the ineffable beauty of their right to live as they chose.

Monte felt his dick getting hard, then harder, and then really boney. He was elated by its need.

"When I first saw you just now," Swiftie said, "I thought you was done for. What the hell have you been up to?"

"Trying to get up Kaiser, that's what!"

"You nit," Swiftie said. "You ain't even been up Ziggedy Ridge lately."

"No, but I been up his sister!" They chuckled in awakened sexuality.

The day had dissolved around them and the awe of the bush was cloaking them. They heard the churn of Black Douggie's old bomb of a bike.

"Swiftie?"

"What?"

"Don't take me to a doctor or to hospital. Take me straight home to Grandad."

"Okay, mate. Whatever you say."

Whatever you say, mate! That night somewhere in the Lillipilli Valley there probably were two young girls, who most likely did not know each other, whose marriages and futures depended on this binding teenage alliance. Their loves would be secondary to a matchless mateship that could burn intensely for at least twenty years, engulfing patterns, provisions and promises, barring nothing except the next beer at the next pub; all other certitudes irrelevant beside: " 'E's me mate."

Exit

ONE DAY IN THE ASPECT of another time Monte Howard arrived home with tears in his eyes. Public, cheek-promoted tears. He couldn't stop crying and he couldn't speak, so went to the kitchen sink and splashed cold water in his disgracing face.

"Richard? What is it?" His wife used an old ploy of Grandad's.

"I . . . I feel so stupid. I've been crying all the way home. I . . ."

"Has anything happened to Grandad? Please tell me what it is."

He shook his head. "No. He's OK. He'll be back this weekend. I . . . it's just that . . . on the radio . . . on the way home . . . I heard that . . . Mont . . . Montgomery Clift killed himself . . . and I just started to cry. You won't understand."

"If you'll try me out on that, I'll try." She put soft fingers into his elbow and led him to the chrome-legged table.

"It doesn't matter. Oh, Christ . . . I'm glad there was no one else in the car today. If he'd died . . . or been killed by someone else . . . but to go and kill himself. Why? I just bloodywell started to cry and couldn't stop. It's ridiculous."

"No. It can't be. You're the least ridiculous man in this town."

The kids came in. "What's the matter with Dad?" The boy was slightly aggressive; the little girl looked up with dazzled-kitten eyes.

"He's had bad news about a friend," their mother said quickly, and quietly hand-motioned them to go into the sitting room. They accepted her directions more unquestioningly than usual because they really didn't want to stay there and watch their father cry.

What can a wife say to a husband she has loved dearly for ten years when he loses someone he had loved immensely for over twenty: one of the most handsome young men who ever lived and possibly the greatest actor who ever made a Western, whose photograph he still has in his shirt drawer in a finger-stained brown envelope postmarked Los Angeles?

Knowing she couldn't deliver the sky, she tried for a flickering hope, the stitching kindness in her words as potent as the vapor of fraxinella on a hot night. Considering she was in the middle of getting tea ready, her loving concern almost made up for the initiative she didn't command. "You should be grateful we have the tellie now and you can watch his old movies."

He shook his head angrily, child-stubbornly. "They never show *Red River*."

God forgive her, but she almost smiled before she suggested, "Why don't you have a nice quiet beer while I give the kids a tub *before* we have tea tonight?" It was a miraculous offer from an extra-organized small-town housewife.

"OK."

"You all right?"

"I will be. I'm sorry if I worried you."

"That's all right. You haven't given me such a shock since you came home and told me about . . . Granny Green." She was glad she didn't have to bite her tongue off to avoid mentioning Swiftie's death, which in its tragedy had given their marriage new impetus. Maddo had grown up steamrolling life like a train siphoning itself into a tunnel . . . coming out the dark side with a splash of white thunder.

"Swiftie threw everything into living except his shadow."

His glorious head was shaved from his shoulders in an automobile accident when he was twenty-three. He left a wife and four beautiful kids. It was a stinging, stinking-hot day when they buried him and all the oldies had little plastic battery-operated fans which they played occasionally at their necks, eyes and tears. The young sheilas sweated profusely and bawled abundantly in swooning, un-swanlike groups. Monte could not force himself to go to watch so much life be battered down by shovelfuls of earth; but his wife went, feeling guilty, knowing she would inherit that much more of her husband's time and love and friendship, which could not be taken to the grave.

The Church of England minister said pleasant-ending things but evaded the truth: Terence Madison was one young man who had a limitless supply of whatever it was women of any age and all ages want.

Granny Green was perhaps the only woman in town not hung up on Ty-Power Madison. The archetype tyrant, she had died peacefully at her kitchen table aged one hundred and fifteen years, give or take a few winters. Before her she had a plate of coddled eggs, the shells of which had been finely mashed into the mixture. In her ice chest was a homemade jar of mayonnaise. At least a dozen egg shells had been fragmented in the recipe. Boomeroosters decided the egg shells in her diet were responsible for her longevity.

"She had her own bloody teeth till she was ninety-nine."

"Till the day she died her eyesight was better than most people's with glasses."

"Ya know . . . she made a pretty good wompy from those grapes she used to spit on. Reckon that helped her live longer than Lot?"

It could never be said that Granny Green's spirit ever left Boomeroo, because her undying cockie can still be heard, morning, noon and oftimes night, calling to her across the leagues that separate men from their Maker and women from their inhibiting Eve-guilt in a monotonous voice that echoes like the hereafter: "Give'm-shit-Granny-give'm-shit!" And the kids in Boomeroo still know that, wherever she is, she is doing exactly that.

After tea that heartbreaking night, Monte said to his son, Aaron, "Come on down the ducket with me, Boy. I want to tell you something . . . show you something. Come on! The world didn't come to an end just because I'm not an emotional dwarf. So, I cried? Stiff shit! Come on." He flicked four fingers impatiently.

"Me too?" His daughter had a smile for every word in her limited vocabulary. "Me too, Daddy!"

In a conflicting moment Monte considered his past and her future, and all the bone structure that Grandad and Miss Cruikshank had battled into him bombed his brain. He said, "Sure . . . hell, why not? Come on then, Kathleen . . . hurry . . . before your mother gets too henny and starts cackling." He flicked the fingers on his other hand, beckoning her.

He took his children down to the gardened-over no-man's-land where Corker was buried and showed them the remembered spot, and told them about a pigeon he had loved beyond reality, which had almost made him famous. His daughter, listening far more intently than his son, was somberly engrossed by the tale he told . . . so he went on to tell her about Boadicea as well, while Aaron went to sleep in his fatherly arms.

"Tell me about the cloud again, and about the fat man," she implored.

So he told her again, realizing that she was Corker's future and keeper . . . and the world did not come to an end.

*There's a train leaving Venice at
   dawn;
It goes to Vienna via Trieste,
This train that leaves Venice at dawn.
And the people you meet here
Live on your street . . .
Wherever you live in this world.
They smile with your eyes
And they walk with your feet
And nothing is different at all.
You listen with their ears,
You speak with their hands
And you know their neighbor's
   face . . .
   He is yours!*

*The children are filled with
The love in their days,
And their joy is their only need:
On this train leaving Venice at dawn.
When you get to Vienna . . .
Your heart is reborn
In the same kind of world
That was all yours before:
Before you left Venice at dawn.*

*RADsong
For Callie Gordon*

ABOUT THE AUTHOR

Paul John Radley was born in Newcastle, Australia, in 1962 and attended high school through grade ten. His first novel, *Jack Rivers and Me*, completed a year later, was the first recipient of the Australian/Vogel Literary Award for fiction and was a best seller there in 1981. Acclaimed as an "Australian *Under Milk Wood*," *Jack Rivers* was published by Ticknor & Fields in 1986. *My Blue-Checker Corker and Me* is Paul Radley's second novel; his third, *Good Mates!*, was published in Australia in 1985. Together these novels make up the Boomeroo Trilogy. Paul Radley rooms at the Crown and Anchor Hotel in Newcastle, where he is at work on his fourth novel. He also works part time as a bartender, plays Rugby Union, and "rages" at discos.